I0583726

DINNER AT THE

BLUE MOON CAFE

Rick R. Reed

A NineStar Press Publication

www.ninestarpress.com

Dinner at the Blue Moon Cafe

Copyright © 2020 by Rick R. Reed
Cover Art by Natasha Snow Copyright © 2020

This is a work of fiction. Names, characters, places, and incidents are either the product of the author's imagination or are used fictitiously. Any resemblance to actual persons living or dead, business establishments, events, or locales is entirely coincidental.

All rights reserved. No part of this publication may be reproduced in any material form, whether by printing, photocopying, scanning or otherwise without the written permission of the publisher. To request permission and all other inquiries, contact NineStar Press at the physical or web addresses above or at Contact@ninestarpress.com.

Printed in the USA

Print ISBN: 978-1-64890-114-0

First Edition, October, 2020
Originally Published in March 2010

Also available in eBook, ISBN: 978-1-64890-113-3

WARNING:
This book contains sexually explicit content, which may only be suitable for mature readers, and scenes of graphic violence and gore.

A monster moves through the darkest night, lit only by the full moon, taking them, one by one, from Seattle's gay gathering areas.

In an atmosphere of spine-tingling fear, Thad Matthews finds his first true love cooking in an Italian restaurant called The Blue Moon Cafe. Sam Lupino is everything Thad has ever hoped for in a man: virile, sexy as hell, kind, and...he can cook!

As the pair's love heats up, so do the questions. Who is the killer preying on Seattle's gay men? What secrets is Sam's Sicilian family hiding? And, more important, why do Sam's unexplained disappearances always coincide with the full moon?

When the secrets are finally revealed, is Thad and Sam's love for one another strong enough to weather the horrific revelations revealed by the light of the full moon?

For Bruce, my heart, my soul, my everything.

Prologue

AUGUST

He's hungry. He eyes the full moon above him through a caul of bloodred. The moon shines as brightly as the sun, warming and energizing him, heightening his senses. He "sees" with all of them, but smell predominates. Before him, the streets of Seattle's Capitol Hill neighborhood stand out in sharp detail, silvery and shimmering from the moon's light, making it easy to track potential prey. And in the air, everywhere, are scents—beer, cigarette smoke, the pale fishy tang of Elliot Bay to the west, car exhaust. But underlying all this is sheer bliss. He lifts his snout to savor it: the aroma of human flesh...and blood. Blood pulsing in the bodies of hundreds of carousers out for a Friday night revel, coursing in and out of bars, heedless and unwary, celebrating the beginning of the weekend.

Their heat, movement, voices, and—most of all—scents give him a paradoxically hungry and deliciously tingling feeling of anticipation deep in the pit of his gut.

His leathery black nose quivers, pulling the scent inside, where he can savor it. His pale gray-furred ears point up to the moon, alert, alert for the sound of a man alone, one that's ripe. He wants to howl but knows such a display will draw attention to him as he sits, panting, in an alley behind a Vietnamese restaurant shuttered for the night. Already a pair of men clad in jeans and tight T-shirts have wandered by and peered into the shadows the alley provides, wondering.

"Jesus!" one of them says. "Would you look at that? What is that? Some kind of dog? It's huge!"

His friend leans over, farther into the alley, far enough for the creature to catch the scent of the man's sweat underlying the cologne with which he polluted himself. The sweat makes his mouth water, his stomach growl, and makes him eager to pounce.... But he knows he must be patient. The night affords plenty of time to hunt.

Reward must always be balanced by careful calculation of risk.

"Yeah, dude. I think it's a German shepherd...or a husky. Somethin' like that. Come on, let's get to the Cuff."

"I thought we were going to Neighbours."

"The Cuff has hotter guys."

The men hurry off, unaware of how appetizing they are, how close they edged to their own demise.

He licks his chops and stares up at the moon as a cloud passes over, partially obscuring its radiance.

He has time to wait. Time to let the scents, sounds, and sights of the lively August night ramp up his hunger, his need, making the resulting feast all that much more succulent. There are practical reasons, too, for his patience. "In the Wee Small Hours" (as the song goes), there will be fewer witnesses to his impromptu alfresco supper of flesh and blood. The few people out—his prey—are more likely to be intoxicated and careless of heading down an alley just like the one in which he now crouches, waiting, every sense on alert.

Intoxicated...

Before dawn creeps up over the Cascade Mountains, he knows he'll be intoxicated. That, and utterly satisfied. He circles a few times and lies down beside a dumpster.

*

He's dozed off. When he awakens, the air is cooler and the night quieter. The sounds of traffic, laughter, and voices have diminished to almost nothing. The rush of wind ruffles his fur as he gets to all fours, raising his snout to test the air.

Yes. There are humans close by. Two. He smells their perspiration and, beneath that, their blood. Their warmth rides to him like a delicious current on the night breeze. He stands quietly, heart rate quickening, muscles tensing, tracking them. They are just outside the alley in which he waits and are making noises, not talking. But there are definite sounds. He moves forward, silent on black paws, to the alley's mouth. In a darkened doorway, he hears the sound of human mating—grunts, groans, and sighs. He sniffs, calculating. There are two men, one of them older, not as healthy, and one young, vigorous.

Boldly he trots out of the alley and crosses the street to watch from between two parked cars. The men don't even notice; they are so absorbed in what they're doing, and he's so full of stealth that he might as well be a ghost gliding through the night.

The pair occupies the doorway of a storefront, cloaked in shadow. Human eyes, passing by, would not even register their existence. But he can see them. The younger one, the one for whom he is already licking his chops, stands before the older one, jeans pushed down to his knees. His shirt is pulled up over his shoulders and behind his neck, exposing exquisite musculature and a constellation of inked skin. Throwing his head back, the young man whispers rapidly how "fuckin' good" it all feels, while the older man kneels in front of him, his head bobbing up and down at his crotch.

The act takes fewer than ten minutes. The scent of sweat and semen hangs in the air. The older man rises, looks around, stuffs himself back inside his pants, and zips. He glances around again, although the creature can't imagine why—there's no one else to witness anything—and takes out his wallet. He digs in it, pulls out a few bills, and hands them to the younger man, the one with the shaved head, the bulging muscles, and the tattoos. The younger man snatches the money away and smiles. "Thanks." He stuffs the money into his jeans pocket.

The older man begins to walk away, and the younger one grabs his arm. "No kiss goodbye?"

They both laugh. The older man pecks the younger on his mouth. At the same time, the younger man pulls him closer as if to embrace him and reaches back, smoothly pulling the wallet from the older man's pants. The other man, unaware, hurries off into the night toward downtown.

"Muscles" counts the money, chuckling, then rifles through the wallet.

He hears the young man whisper, "What story will you make up for wifey about how you lost your wallet?" He throws back his head and laughs out loud at the thought. He pulls the remaining cash from the wallet, extracts a couple of credit cards, and tosses the wallet to the ground.

The creature takes him in with all his senses. He's perfect.

He tracks his prey through the streets, uphill. He begins to question whether luck will be on his side when the man ducks into an alley. He follows, amused that, after all these blocks, the man has never once noticed him so close behind. The beast stares as his prey pulls out his dick and sprays a bright yellow stream on the brick wall before him. The scent of piss drifts over, ammonia-like, but it's part of the man's essence and his heat. Mixed in with the smell of it is also the scent of his semen, left over from his prior business transaction.

Drool runs from the creature's mouth. He can wait no longer. He pounces, and without a howl, without a growl, without even a bark, he is upon him.

Tearing.

The man doesn't even have time to scream.

Chapter One

Music from his clock radio woke Thad Matthews at 6:00 a.m. The song, "Smokestack Lightning," yanked him from a heavy, dream-laden sleep. Its energy forced his eyes open wider, caused synapses, eight hours dormant, to tingle, and made him want to move. Nonetheless, he slapped at the snooze button, silencing the bluesy wail, rolled over, and then pulled the comforter over his head. He was glad he had tuned his clock radio to KPLU, Seattle's only all-blues all-the-time station, but he desperately wanted to recapture just a few more minutes of his dream, in which he'd found himself on the moors of England. All he could recall was that the moors themselves were appropriately fog shrouded and lit with a silvery luminance from above. Someone waited for him in the shadows and fog. And he couldn't, for the life of him, know for certain if that someone meant to do him harm or meant to just *do* him.

He'd been having a lot of sexual dreams lately.

As much as he wanted to unravel the mystery of the dream—and to perhaps savor the vague sexual vibrations he was getting from it—sleep eluded him. He found thoughts of the day crowding in, preventing even the most remote possibility of a recurrence of slumber.

Thad sat up in the four-poster, rubbing his eyes like a little boy, and wondered why he bothered setting an alarm. He had no job to go to, no pressing engagements, no muse to answer to—hell, he didn't even have an appointment for an oil change.

This day, like all his others, stretched out before him completely unmarred with obligations other than the requirements life imposed upon him, such as eating and going to the bathroom, which the erection poking up under his sheets compelled him to take care of. He called this morning wood a pee-on, because once he had put that particular need to rest, it most often subsided.

After stumbling to the adjoining bathroom and letting go with a flow that caused a mighty sigh of relief to issue forth from him, he thought once again that maybe today should be the day he looked harder into getting himself some employment—anything to put him into contact with other people and to fill his waking hours. Lord knew he filled out enough applications and answered enough Help Wanted ads on Craigslist to keep the officials down at unemployment sending him checks. But all his efforts, dishearteningly, were ignored.

It had been nearly four months since he had been laid off at Perk, the national chain of coffee shops headquartered in suburban Shoreline. Thad had been there for six years, in the marketing department, spending his days writing clever sayings for paper coffee cups and point-of-purchase signs for the stores. It was a tough job, but someone had to do it. And writing phrases like "Plan on Being Spontaneous" paid the bills, even if it didn't provide much creative or intellectual challenge. It helped sell coffee, and Thad never kidded himself: that's why he was employed there.

Except now they didn't need him anymore. Who would write the signs for their special Iced Coffee blend?

He gazed down at the bubbling golden froth in the toilet and flushed it away, along with his thoughts about his former job. He turned and rinsed his hands under the sink, then splashed cold water on his face. Standing up straight, he stared at his reflection in the medicine cabinet mirror.

"You're too young for a life of leisure," he said to his reflection, rubbing his hands through his short, coarse red hair, which stuck up in a multitude of directions. People paid good money for products that would make their hair look as fetchingly disheveled as Thad's did right now. He peered closer at himself, taking inventory of his pale skin, his gray eyes, and the constellation of freckles that spanned his nose and the tops of his cheeks. He flexed, thinking he was looking a little flabby around the middle.

"Workout day. I'll head over to the gym today. I need it." He sucked in his gut and let it out again, thinking it was empty and needed refilling. A Pagliacci delivery pizza only went so far. His slumber and active dream life, he supposed, had all but digested the pie.

Thad moved to the bedroom and began tossing pillows on the floor to make up his bed. He wasn't sure why he bothered with this either, since it was unlikely anyone would see the military-neat bed except for him, when he would approach it once more this evening just to mess it all up again. But it was important to Thad to have a routine. Otherwise his days would blend into one meaningless chunk of time, formless, without definition or purpose.

It was becoming increasingly hard enough to distinguish Tuesday from Thursday—or Sunday, for that matter.

Back when he was putting in forty-plus hours a week, he envied the increasing number of friends and acquaintances who had gotten laid off during the economic downturn. The money they made on unemployment seemed like enough—at least for him and his modest lifestyle in his Green Lake studio apartment—and the freedom they had seemed worth the cut in pay.

But now he wasn't so sure. The uncertainty of what would happen if he still wasn't working when the unemployment checks dwindled down to zero hung over him like a vague threat. And the freedom wasn't really so great, when that same threat prevented him from spending much money, lest he should need it down the road for luxuries like food and a roof over his head.

Worst of all was what the job loss had done to his self-esteem. Thad needed some meaning in his life, a purpose. That much had been instilled in him since he was a little boy, back in Chicago growing up in the working class neighborhood of Bridgeport, where his father was a cop and his mother waited tables at a Lithuanian restaurant.

He pulled on a T-shirt and a pair of sweatpants, padded out to the office area of his apartment, and plopped down in front of his laptop. He planned to check out the classifieds on Craigslist, then Monster, then CareerBuilder. When he was first laid off, he looked only at writing and editing jobs but had lately broadened his search to include, well, just about everything. Thad realized he would work retail, man a customer service phone line, groom dogs, or wait tables, as long as he had a job.

Yet the rest of the world hadn't gotten wind of his eagerness to accept any kind of employment. Or if they had, they weren't saying.

Before he went through the often-depressing ritual of cyber pavement pounding, he would check out what had happened in the world since he had stumbled in last night from an evening of self-consolation and vodka on Capitol Hill. He hit the little orange-and-blue Firefox icon on the dock at the bottom of his screen to bring up the day's online news...

And was jolted right out of whatever sluggishness he was feeling. He stared at the lead article for that day's *Seattle Post-Intelligencer*. A chill coursed through him, and he slowly shook his head as he read the details of that morning's top story, titled "Brutal Slaying in Capitol Hill." The article described how an as-yet-unidentified young man had been killed in an alley in the Seattle neighborhood known for its heavy concentration of gay bars and clubs. Thad had to stop reading for a moment to close his eyes because the gruesome details were simply too much to bear. His stomach churned. The man had not just been killed but had been literally ripped apart. Very little blood was found at the scene. And forensics had already determined that there was no trace of metal found on the victim's flesh, which meant that the deed had to have been done with something other than a knife. The worst detail of all was the fact that the remains bore definite signs that much of the man's flesh had been eaten. Authorities are keeping details to themselves regarding who—or what—the perpetrator could have been. The story closed with the usual cautions about what to do— don't travel alone, avoid strangers and unlit places—when something so unsettling and violent occurs.

Thad exited Firefox sooner than he had planned and stared out the window. His heart thumped in his chest. Bile splashed at the back of his throat and a cold sweat broke out on his forehead. He had been in Capitol Hill the night before, having a dirty martini or three at Neighbours, one of the gay ghetto's most popular hangouts. He wondered if, as he had made his way back to the bus stop, he had passed the killer or killers. If perhaps the killer or killers had eyed *him*, wondering if he would suffice for their demented purposes. He could see himself through their eyes, being watched from the shadows of a vestibule or an alley as he made his way back to the bus stop on Broadway. He wondered if he looked appetizing. He had been told on more than one occasion that he was "tasty" and "delicious," but those doing the describing were not thinking of him as dinner—at least not in the conventional sense. He wondered if perhaps the only thing that had saved him was the coincidental passing of a boisterous group from the University of Washington, coming up alongside him just as the fiend in the dark was ready to pounce. He shivered. For once, rejection was a comforting thought.

Rejection, under these circumstances, was the new "getting lucky."

Still, some poor soul had not been as lucky as he had, and today forensics was probably busy trying to figure out just who this unfortunate soul was. From what Thad had read, it didn't sound like they had much to go on. Dental records, maybe? What kind of animal would not only kill a fellow human being but also eat his flesh and drink his blood? Was this a human being at all? Thad had heard of bears occasionally making their misguided ways down from the mountains and into Seattle, but they usually got no farther than suburban parks and backyards. And the "bears" that routinely cruised the Capitol Hill neighborhood were of a much more cuddly variety.

Surely, though, an *animal* couldn't have been roaming around busy Capitol Hill on Friday night. The neighborhood, on weekend nights, was a blur of barhoppers and partiers, its hilly streets filled with people and cars jockeying for position. Loud and well lit, it was the kind of neighborhood that would scare the shit out of an animal, at least an animal with normal fears and inclinations. This had to be the work of a person, or people, right? And whoever was behind such a thing had to be majorly warped. Thad had a quick vision of pale-gray eyes and enormous canine teeth until he banished the imagery to the back of his brain, grateful for another kind of canine distraction.

That distraction had just sidled up beside Thad, her arrival signaled by a clicking of toenails on hardwood. Thad glanced down at his gray-and-white Chihuahua, Edith, staring up at him with her dark eyes. Her tongue stuck out one side of her mouth, giving her a both comical and wizened appearance. The dog was about a hundred years old, and Thad thought, for better or worse, she was his very best friend in the world. Edith got up on her hind legs to paw at Thad's lap, indicating to him that he was not the only creature in the house that had to pee first thing in the morning.

Thad got up and, with Edith following impatiently behind, slid into flip-flops and grabbed her leash. "C'mon, sweetheart, let's take a little walk down to the lake, and then we'll see about getting us both some breakfast."

*

Saturday passed much as Monday had, and Tuesday, and Wednesday, and so on. In other words, Thad cleaned his studio apartment that didn't need cleaning; updated his

Facebook status five times and his Twitter status three—stealing quotes from Lily Tomlin and Kathy Griffin to make himself sound more witty than he was; searched on Facebook for several hours for old friends, relatives, classmates, and boyfriends; made tuna salad for lunch—half the can of Chicken of the Sea went to Edith, who seduced him out of it with her eyes—and streamed three episodes of *True Blood* on his laptop.

By six o'clock Thad was staring out the window and thinking about counting his freckles, just for something to do. Perhaps he could shave the hair between his eyebrows? Do another online crossword? Google himself again?

"I gotta get out of here, money or no money." He glanced down at Edith, who was lying at the opposite end of the couch. She looked up at him as if she understood and then glanced over at the door.

"That's right, sweetheart. Daddy needs to get out...at least for a little dinner." Thad had just gotten a flyer in the mail the day before, describing a new place that had opened on Green Lake Way called the Blue Moon Café. He had gone by it several times during his runs around the lake and watched as the restaurant had slowly come together: one day kitchen equipment was delivered, another it was dark-cherry tables and chairs, still another a shipment of beer and wine. Yet he had no idea, really, what kind of cuisine they'd serve.

But one thing Thad had loved about the Green Lake neighborhood when he moved in was its abundance of stores, restaurants, pubs, and cafés within walking distance. Thad had never owned a car and didn't want one. So he liked to support the businesses there, even though many of them were more geared toward families and couples than the livelier—and gayer—Capitol Hill neighborhood, ten or fifteen minutes away depending on traffic.

After serving Edith her dinner of Thad's own special blend of brown rice, chicken, and peas and carrots, Thad hit the shower. He took a long time under the hot spray, washing and conditioning his hair, soaping every orifice, and shaving the hair on his balls and adjacent to his penis, revealing his manhood in its most flattering light. Even in Green Lake and even on an outing for a quiet meal, one never knew whom one would meet. Besides, Thad had all the time in the world.

Don't remind me, he thought, sliding his head under the shower to rinse the conditioner from his ginger hair.

He dressed in a pair of black jeans, combat boots, and a vintage Cockney Rejects T-shirt he'd found a couple of weeks ago at Value Village. He worked a dollop of hair wax through his hair, making it stand on end fetchingly and giving him that just-out-of-bed look. Although he hadn't made it to the gym that day, the black made him look thinner and made his shoulders, naturally broad, stand out. The thin cotton fabric also clung alluringly to his pecs.

He thought briefly that he should head to Capitol Hill instead, or even the University District just east of him, but Thad was the kind of guy who, once he had made a plan, stuck to it.

He took Edith out for a quick bathroom break, kissed the top of her head, and set off for the Blue Moon Café. His step was light, and he'd set his status on Facebook to "optimistic."

Who knew what the night would bring?

Chapter Two

From the moment Thad stepped through the front door of the Blue Moon Café, the décor cleared up any mystery about what kind of food they served. The little café, with its mahogany bar along one wall, its grouping of maybe a dozen tables, and its faux-tin ceiling, could have been straight out of central casting for "Italian joint." Thad saw the requisite checkered tablecloths, the oil paintings of Italian landmarks like the canals of Venice, the Coliseum, the Leaning Tower of Pisa, and St. Peter's Square. And yes, each table sported a candle plugged into the opening of an empty green-glass Chianti bottle. A TV sat above the bar, thankfully turned off.

"Buona Sera" by Louis Prima played from the overhead speaker system. Thad was certain the rest of the evening would be peppered with the likes of Dean Martin, Jerry Vale, Rosemary Clooney, and of course, Sinatra. Underneath the music was the usual restaurant orchestra: conversation, laughter, the clink of glassware, and the tinkle of silverware.

The scents of garlic, oregano, basil, and tomatoes perfumed the air. Over a counter at the rear of the restaurant, Thad could see into the kitchen: a wood-burning oven, chefs busy at their stations, the occasional upsurge of flame as one of them poured alcohol into a pan and ignited it by tipping the pan. Thad's mouth began to water.

He already liked this place.

And he liked it even more when he saw the bartender, who was busy drying wineglasses and reaching up to hang them upside down on a rack above the bar. He was a compact little guy, olive skin and shaved head. His muscles tested the endurance of the black T-shirt he wore, and even from his vantage near the hostess stand, Thad could make out the thick black five o'clock shadow that covered his jaw. He was just the kind of guy Thad fantasized about. One who would take him roughly and be in charge.

Stop it, now! I'm in Green Lake, not Capitol Hill. This guy probably has a wife and two kids at home and would not appreciate I'm imagining how he would look should the seams of that tight T-shirt burst and reveal a defined and hairy chest. He wouldn't cotton at all to my thoughts of wondering how his asshole would taste, for cryin' out loud.

Or maybe he would...

Thad grinned and bounced up and down a couple of times on his heels, feeling strangely energized and definitely a little smitten.

Shut up, horndog. Behave yourself.

As if the bartender had heard him, he looked up at Thad standing by the door. Thad realized he was looking at the guy in a way not all that different from the way Edith would eye a filet mignon. He couldn't quite be sure, but if some telepathy had taken place, the guy was not flattered. He wasn't smiling. In fact, there was something surly and challenging about the look he gave Thad that caused his buoyant mood to wither.

"Someone will be right with you. Or if you wanna come over to the bar, I can make you somethin'." His voice was gravelly deep and had a trace of an Italian accent. In spite of the bartender's obvious lack of interest and perhaps even a touch of homophobia, Thad was, nevertheless, still charmed.

He nodded at the bartender and shifted his gaze to a new object of adoration and lust, heading right toward him. *What? Me, fickle?* Thad grinned at his own hormones and wondered if they suffered from attention deficit disorder.

But the man making his way across the small space, most likely the proprietor, head chef, whatever, made Thad forget all about the bartender and his stubbly face. This man was even more Thad's cup of *T*...and that *T* stood for testosterone.

Clad in a crisp white shirt and black pants, the man wore an apron sashed around his middle and the most welcoming smile Thad had ever laid eyes on. He was a big bear of a man, not so much in height—Thad estimated him at about five foot ten—but in sheer bulk and mass. He was not fat by any means, but his shoulders were broad, and his arms looked like tree trunks, straining against even the loose white cotton of his shirt. He had rolled up his sleeves, probably to work, but to Thad he had rolled them up to show off the thick coat of coarse black hair that covered his forearms. Curly black hair peeked out from his collar. And his face! There was no mistaking: this guy was from Southern Italy. He had the big nose and full lips and the rich olive complexion. He sported a thick black beard, well trimmed. When his eyes met Thad's, Thad all but melted into the floor. They were the darkest irises Thad had probably ever seen, so brown they were almost black. The guy's pupils all but disappeared in them. Thad could think only of dark chocolate. Well, actually he could think of a lot of other things.

He barely had the breath to croak out, "Table for one?"

"Prego!" The man said, nearing him and smiling even more broadly. "Of course. You will follow me, okay?"

Anywhere. Thad walked behind his host and was not too proud to check out how his black pants gripped his high-riding ass. An ass that could probably be used to set a tray of cocktails on, should the need arise.

Thad was all bottom, but he could appreciate a nice *culo*. He was grateful he knew a little Italian. He hoped to learn a lot more...and soon.

The man led him toward a small two-top in the back of the restaurant and pulled out a chair. Their eyes met, and Thad, a firm believer in the language of the eyes, was completely taken aback when he detected that the interest he felt in this man was mutual. Thad grinned and knew he probably looked as stupid as Edith with her tongue lolling out one side of her little mouth.

He didn't care.

"Grazie." Thad sat down. "That's right, isn't it? That's Italian for 'thank you,' huh?"

"You are right, sir. But we like our customers to speak English here, okay? Keeps them—and us—out of trouble later on, like when they order something not on the menu but on a woman, by mistake." He grinned. The man's velvety voice penetrated Thad and made his nerve endings quiver.

And it gave him a hard-on. He blushed.

"You never been to the Blue Moon before, no?"

"No. You guys just opened, right? I run around the lake a few times a week, and I watched as you got set up."

"So this is your first time?"

Thad wanted to laugh but instead reined in his stupid, lustful grin just a bit and nodded. "Yes, but I've been dying to try what you have to offer." *Jesus! You can call me Blanche Devereaux!*

"Will you permit me to, eh, try something a little different with you?"

Thad couldn't help but smile, and his thoughts shifted to about a hundred "different" things the host would be more than welcome to try with him. The funny thing was, none of them involved food.

"I see by your smile you like my idea."

Thad nodded. He felt like an idiot. When had his capacity to form words disappeared?

"I just give you a little taste of where I'm from, okay? I came over from Sicily a bit more than a year ago and just moved to Seattle a couple of months ago. But I think you're gonna love my food. It's not the typical stuff you get at these Italian restaurants around here. You ain't gonna find no spaghetti and meatballs here! No sir! I make good Sicilian food, the kind country people eat." The guy winked at Thad. "The kind that satisfies, you know?"

"Oh, I know." Thad grinned. He was charmed by this big, overflowing lump of Italian masculinity, his black hair, his warm eyes, the way he made such a game attempt at speaking English.

"So you just sit back, relax, and let Sam take care of you, okay?"

"Okay, Sam." Their eyes met, and Thad thought, now that he knew his host's name, he should offer his own. Before Sam could leave the table, Thad stuck out a paw. "Hey, by the way, I'm Thad. I just live a couple blocks over. You treat me right and I'll be back for more."

Sam raised one bushy eyebrow. He might not have been an expert English speaker yet, but Thad could tell from the gazes they exchanged that the man was fluent in the language of innuendo.

Sam grasped Thad's hand warmly and firmly, and the pair shook hands just a beat longer than two straight guys would do it. And two straight males would have never made eye contact the way the two of them did: intense and held for the entire duration of the handshake.

Once again, Thad felt a paradoxically delicious yet uncomfortable tightening in his jeans.

Rosemary Clooney was belting out "Mambo Italiano" when Sam brought over the first course. "We start with something special. In Sicily, this is street food, but I think that here...it's something, um, a little different?" Sam set a plate before him. "This is *arancini di riso con ricott'*." Thad noticed how Sam dropped the last vowel off "ricotta" and wondered if that was part of his dialect. Sam gestured with open hands toward the plate, upon which sat three golden balls of deep fried rice on a bed of fresh basil leaves. "I make these just for you. You tell me how you like, and if you think they're good, I add them to the menu."

"What are they, exactly?" Whatever the answer to that question, Thad knew they were going to be spectacular.

"They're balls I make from rice, filled with ricott' and spinach. Then we roll in fresh breadcrumbs, parmigiano, and deep fry. *Delizioso!*"

And they were. As was the rest of the meal...pastina—tiny pasta—simmered in chicken broth with parmesan and roasted butternut squash, flavored with onion and thyme; and then a simple roasted chicken half and new potatoes dressed with olive oil, garlic, and fresh basil, with a side of broccoli; and finally, a simple olive oil cake with marionberries and powdered sugar. "We're not too big on dessert in Sicily," Sam explained, "but when I moved here to Washington, I tried the marionberries and fell in love."

The strong espresso that came with dessert set Thad's nerve endings to tingling but gave him the staying power to remain at his table until closing. He was a man with a plan. And Sam didn't seem to mind him whiling away the hours at his little table, stopping by to bring him a grappa, then another, then another, explaining that he made the fermented brandy himself, just like "his papa used to."

By the end of the evening, Thad was feeling giddy and drunk, and not just because of the grappa. If Sam had not been flirting with him all night, then Thad had the intuition of an armchair.

Finally the parade of Italy's greatest hits came to a close, to be replaced by softer strains of a Verdi opera, turned low. The restaurant emptied, and the overhead lights came on, casting a brighter glare on the room, yet it still managed to look homespun and comfortable. Thad wondered if this was all some sort of interior designer plan or if it just happened, based on Sam's memories of his homeland. Thad had the feeling he was being accorded even more special treatment, because the place was officially closed, signaled by the busboy turning the little sign in the window around so that now "Open" faced the restaurant interior.

Where would the night go? Outside, the foot traffic along Green Lake Way had slowed. Certainly, throughout the evening, Sam had made his interest clear with lingering gazes, a firm touch on Thad's hand or a squeeze of his shoulder as he passed by, and comments like how Sam had a weakness for red hair.

Thad was pretty certain that if he invited Sam home with him, he would accept. But Thad wasn't sure he wanted to taint the magic of this night by cheapening it into a one-night stand. Wouldn't it be better to wait for sex, to build the anticipation, to let it happen after they had gotten to know each other better? His hormones and his sentimental side were at continual war throughout the evening, once Thad knew for sure that Sam reciprocated his feelings of nearly overwhelming attraction.

At age twenty-four, Thad wasn't surprised that his hormones were beating his more romantic side to a pulp.

In the end, Thad knew there was no contest. He just hoped that if Sam followed him home, it would mean the kindling of a flame that would only continue to burn more brightly. He wanted to see him again. Never before had Thad felt himself so powerfully drawn to not only to a guy's looks, which were smoldering, but to his warmth, kindness, and sense of humor. And the fact that his cooking was on a plane akin to art didn't hurt either. A man who could satisfy all his appetites wasn't too much to ask for, was it?

Thad began to worry when Sam didn't join him at his table after a half hour or so had passed. In fact, Sam had vanished into the kitchen, and it was clear that the grappa had been cut off.

Thad, in spite of his youth and bad-little-boy good looks, wrestled with feelings of inadequacy and self-esteem, just like almost everyone else. And when he wanted something as badly as he wanted Sam, the paranoia within him rose in direct proportion to his desire.

So he was greatly relieved, after he watched the bartender exit, locking the door behind him, that Sam finally reemerged from the kitchen with a glass of red wine and stood next to Thad's table, looking down at him. Or should that be leering down at him? Sam wore a lopsided grin that was almost feral. Thad loved it.

"I'm off duty. I'm just me now...Sam. Do you mind if I join you?"

Thad noticed that, although Sam's Italian accent was still there, it was diminished...and he didn't speak quite like the guy just off the boat anymore. As if reading his mind, Sam smiled and said, "I play up the Italian a bit when I'm in owner mode. I hope you don't think I was being deceitful."

"Not at all. I'm sure it's good for business."

"We'll see." Sam pulled out the chair across from him and sat down, stretched out, and rested one of his legs on top of Thad's. He leaned close. "I'm not really thinking about business anymore." The intensity of Sam's gaze was a magnet, pulling Thad toward him almost irresistibly. "You know?"

"I know," Thad breathed. Blood had been rushing steadily to his face and lower, and if much more of the stuff made its way north or south, he feared he might explode. Thad knew he was faced with two options: one—do the socially correct thing and sit there, sipping drinks and making polite chitchat for about a half hour, artfully working his way up to an invitation to a stroll around the lake, which then might morph into stopping by his place for a drink, or two—simply lay his cards on the table and hope for the best.

Because patience had never been one of his virtues, the latter option won out. He looked around the room and discovered, to his surprise, that it was completely empty, stood a little, leaned over the table, and kissed Sam. What surprised him was how hungrily Sam accepted the kiss, grabbing the back of Thad's neck roughly to pull him closer. His beard scratched against Thad's skin, the sensation strangely irritating and hot, all at once. Sam's tongue forced Thad's lips apart and dove inside, exploring, making Thad dizzy and giving him a taste of red wine and echoes of garlic and tomatoes. Sam pulled him closer, so that Thad's upper body lay sprawled across the tabletop. The Chianti bottle candleholder toppled over and crashed to the floor. Neither paid it any mind. The hungry kiss was the culmination of an entire evening of longing glances, double entendres, and fleeting touches, all of them combining to stoke a fire neither knew was being kindled until their lips met and it burst into flame.

Finally Thad pulled himself away, shuddering with the delicious sensations coursing through him. Breathless, he thought if the kiss had gone on just a little longer and with just a bit more ferocity, he would have had a mess in his briefs to clean up. And he wanted to save every drop of that "mess" for Sam.

In the end there were no clever seductive phrases available for Thad to employ. He simply looked at Sam, who was as breathless as he, and said, "Wanna come home with me?"

"Let's go." Sam pulled Thad up roughly by his arm. Thad didn't mind a bit. Sam bit his neck, licked his ear, and whispered, "I'm an animal in bed. Are you sure?"

Dumbly, Thad could only nod and hope his knees would hold out for the short walk to his apartment. His heart thudded in his chest.

Outside, the cold night air was a shock to Thad's lust-tempered skin. He wanted to hurry and pulled Sam along by his hand. Their first time, he had a feeling, would be savage and over quickly, but they had all night, right?

As they headed to his apartment, Thad's anticipation was withered just a fraction by an odd sensation. Even though the streets of the Green Lake neighborhood were still at this late night hour, and even though the wind rustled the leaves on the trees, Thad had that prickly sensation that someone was watching.

He glanced all around him and saw nothing.

Thad shrugged and pulled Sam in for another kiss. "It'll only take about five minutes to get home."

Sam growled, "Five minutes too long. Let's hurry."

Chapter Three

In his imagination, Thad pictured the two of them coming in his front door and Sam throwing him roughly up against the door, covering his face and neck with kisses while his hands roamed, tweaking a nipple there, fondling his balls here. In the pregnant darkness, the man would work Thad into a frenzy of carnal desire so great he didn't know if they would make it to the bedroom or if they would consummate their passion right on the living room floor. He saw their muscles, slicked with sweat, working in unison like a machine to bring each other to dizzying heights of pleasure.

He hadn't pictured Edith greeting them at the door and the poor Chihuahua manically jumping on him, whining to be taken outside—immediately. So, with reluctance, Thad flipped on the overhead light so he could find her leash. He looked back at Sam, who waited outside in the shadows. "You can just go on in and have a seat on the couch. She won't take more than a minute."

"It's okay. I can wait out here." Sam groped in his pocket and brought out a pack of Marlboro Reds. He extracted one, lit it, and exhaled a plume of blue-gray smoke into the night air. Thad was both repelled and aroused by the sight of Sam lighting up.

Ugh. A smoker. Something I'll have to work on changing. He then couldn't deny the "bad boy" thrill the sight of Sam smoking gave him. *Or maybe not.*

Thad ducked back in and stooped to affix harness and leash to Edith, who was all but hopping up and down with impatience. She whimpered and stared desperately up at him.

"I know. I know," Thad soothed. "Small bladder."

The two stepped outside, and Edith froze when she saw Sam. Her eyes widened, and the hackles along her neck and back went up. She immediately began a furious yapping, baring her teeth and lunging toward Sam, her tiny frame testing the endurance of the leather leash. Thad was surprised the old girl had so much fury and strength within her seven-pound frame. He sent a weak smile Sam's way to apologize for her behavior. "I don't know what's up with her. She's usually not like this."

"Maybe it's the dark. I'll move over here." Sam hurried back down the walkway until he stood near the street, the orange tip of his cigarette glowing in the dark.

Thad squatted down to comfort the little dog shaking with fury and what seemed like terror. He had acquired Edith as a puppy and had made sure she was well socialized from about eight weeks old, taking her everywhere with him and exposing her, over the years, to all sorts of people, other dogs, and even cats. He had never seen her behave like this. *Great! I finally find a man I think I could be nuts about and my dog doesn't like him. Something else I'll have to work on.* Thad walked Edith in the opposite direction from Sam, and she calmed down enough to reestablish her original goal and take care of it.

"I'll put her in the bathroom," Thad called to Sam as he headed back to the apartment. "Give me just a sec. I'll leave the door open, and then you can come in."

Thad grabbed her little shearling bed and put it in the corner of the bathroom. He then rushed into the kitchen to put some peanut butter in her Kong toy. He presented it to her. "Here, I've been nice to you. Now you be nice to me. No more trouble from you." He took one last glance back at the dog, busy with getting peanut butter out of her toy, before closing the bathroom door.

Sam leaned against his front door, smiling. He didn't look tired in the least, even though it was near two in the morning, and he had worked all evening. The color in his cheeks was high, his lips full and slightly parted, and the way he stared at Thad was all invitation. Thad simply wanted to get lost in that big, furry body.

But he was still a little flustered. "Sorry about that. She isn't usually so unfriendly. I don't know what got into her."

"Don't worry about it. I'm not much of a dog person—maybe she knew that. And maybe you don't know what's gotten into her, but I have an inkling you have a very good idea what's going to be getting into you." Sam winked and then laughed.

"You dog!" Thad crossed the room, flicked off the lights, and pressed his body against Sam. The kisses commenced, against the door, just as he had imagined. Thad was, for once, grateful he didn't have a job to go to come Monday morning, because he knew his face would be red and chafed from the pressure of Sam's beard. This way, he imagined he would smile with fond memories every time he looked in a mirror.

They kissed for what seemed like the next hour, until both of them panted and half their faces were damp with each other's saliva. Without their ever leaving the front door, shirts had been undone and pulled apart, flies opened, and shoes kicked into corners.

Breathlessly, Thad forced himself away from Sam and said the three little words every man longs to hear: "To the bed." He grabbed Sam and tugged him toward the bed that occupied one corner of his studio. They fell upon it, laughing and continuing to tear at each other's clothes.

Sam pinned Thad's arms to the sheets and above Thad's head as he bent to cover his upper torso with kisses, tongue laps, and bites that toed the line between pleasure and pain. But Thad, while he might have sighed and even cried out, never complained. He liked his nipples chewed on, and one had to go pretty far to make it too rough. There seemed to be an electric wire inside him, connecting his nipples to his genitals. He squirmed beneath Sam, coherent enough to wonder how this man, whom he had known for only a few hours, seemed to be an expert at what pleased him and the topography of Thad's body.

Sam's head dipped lower, and then lower, until he was at Thad's feet. Thad closed his eyes and kept his arms above his head, grabbing onto the posts in the headboard for support. "Oh yeah," he whimpered as Sam took his toes in his mouth, sucking hard. Slowly Sam made his way along his runner-muscled legs, nipping and kissing his way up. When he took Thad completely inside his mouth, the heat and wet just about made Thad come, but he held on, thinking of Edith's sweet face to keep himself from hurtling over that edge.

Just as he thought he would be unable to hang on any longer and would explode in Sam's mouth, the man stopped and moved up, covering Thad's lean, muscled body with his own like a big, furry blanket.

Muffled, from beneath him, Thad whispered happily, "I could stay like this forever."

"Not quite like this," Sam said, moving back to grab Thad's ankles and push them up on his shoulders. "Like this." Sam positioned himself right at the crack of Thad's ass and smiled down at him.

The heavy beard, the penetrating dark eyes, and the lips parted with lust all combined to make Thad want to cry out "I love you!" but he had the good sense to know it was too soon to make such utterances. Instead, he panted, "There are rubbers and lube in the nightstand drawer."

As Sam moved so he could lean over and open the drawer, Thad glanced down and saw what he would soon be getting. He sucked in his breath and bit his lip, a flurry of quivering desire and, yes, fear coursing through him. Nestled amid a thick mound of black pubic hair rose one of the largest cocks he had ever seen. It must have been eight or nine inches long and only a little less than that dimension in circumference, topped with a huge purple head that made Thad think of plums. The head leaked precum, and Thad had to close his eyes and force himself to breathe more slowly. "Go slow, okay?" he whispered.

And Sam did. He inched himself in a fraction at a time, all the while leaning forward to kiss Thad deeply on the mouth and to tongue and bite his nipples. By the time he was all the way inside, Thad was relaxed and ready. He wiggled down on Sam's cock to get him as far as possible inside him. He pushed at his ass with his legs, throwing caution to the wind, and told him, "You don't have to go slow anymore."

Sam grinned. He didn't go slowly. By the time they finished, the sheets were in a bunch on the floor and both of their bodies glistened with sweat. Even the mattress was wet.

Sam and Thad lay on their backs, breathless. Thad spoke first, but only after several minutes had passed, long enough for him to process what had just happened and to allow his respiration to return to a somewhat normal pace. "That was amazing. I'm no Mary Poppins, but I can honestly say I don't know when it's been that good for me." Thad let out a long, quivering breath. "You're right. You *are* an animal."

Sam laughed, and the sound was comforting, there in the pale, silvery light from a waning moon outside. Thad snuggled into the crook between Sam's chest and arm, resting his head on the fur that blanketed Sam's chest. *This*, he thought, surprising himself, *is just about as good as the sex.*

"I just go with my instincts." Sam stroked Thad's hair gently. "If that makes me an animal, then I'm guilty as charged." He moved slightly away from Thad. "Don't kill me, but do you mind if I have a cigarette? I can go outside if you want."

Thad shook his head, grinning. "A smoke after sex. That's so cliché. But go ahead. Normally I wouldn't allow it, but I'll make an exception for you...Sam." Thad liked how the name felt on his tongue. He leaned over Sam to pull a little tray he had on the nightstand he used for change closer. Sam could use it as an ashtray.

"*Grazie.*" Sam turned to sit up and grope in his pants pocket, bringing out his pack and a lighter. He leaned against the headboard and lit up. The room filled with the acrid stench of burning tobacco and paper, and instead of being repelled as he normally would, Thad moved close to Sam again, taking up his newly claimed spot on the man's chest. He stared up at him, watching him smoke. Lazily he traced circles in the hairy mat covering Sam's chest. His fingers stopped when he caught sight of a design on Sam's left pectoral, something he hadn't noticed in the dim light, or perhaps because it was all but hidden by the forest of hair. Thad got up on one elbow.

"You have a tattoo?"

In the dark, Sam nodded. "I've had it for years, way before tattoos were all the rage like they are these days."

"Especially here in Seattle." Thad often wondered if there was some requirement that all citizens of Seattle must have at least one tattoo. "What's it of?" Thad strained to make out the design's contours in the dim light and couldn't.

Sam leaned forward to switch on the bedside lamp. Thad squinted at the sudden light source, then directed his gaze down at the muscled chest before him. "What is it?" Thad traced the design with his fingers, lowering his head to peer more closely at it. He nipped at Sam's nipple and Sam laughed.

"It's Lupa, the she-wolf who suckled Romulus and Remus, the twins who founded Rome in mythology. Cool, no?" Sam flexed his chest so the wolf seemed to move. Two cherubic twin boys below the figure suckled at her teats.

"It's kind of weird. But it suits you." Thad reached over Sam to turn off the light again. "What brought you to America?"

Did Thad detect a slight stiffening when he asked the question? He had only meant to further their little postcoital conversation. "I don't mean to put you on the spot," he hurried to say, wondering if he had imagined the slight body language. "If it's none of my business, just say so."

Sam relaxed against the bunched-up—and damp—pillows. "No. It's okay. We came from a small village in Sicily. Lots of mountains, rocks, olive trees...not much else. You would probably think it's pretty, but me, I was bored. We just decided one day to go, to come to America, to see if we could make a go of it here. We tried New York City first, but it was too crazy there. Too many people, too expensive. We wanted someplace where everything was not concrete, where there was some nature. Seattle was, how would you say? A natural choice."

Now it was Thad's turn to stiffen just a bit. What was with all the "we" this and "we" that? His feelings, briefly at an all-time high, sunk. Was Sam married? Did he have a lover? Was Thad just that night's side dish? Sam's olive cake with marionberries? Would Sam soon be getting up to hurry home to someone who was sleeping with one eye open, waiting for the sound of his key in the door? Thad didn't want to come off as suspicious, but he couldn't resist his next question and thought he might as well get everything out in the open right from the start.

"You said 'we.' Who's 'we'?" Thad tried to bite his lip to keep himself from saying more, but he couldn't resist the impulse. "Wait. Don't tell me. There's a boyfriend—or a wife—right?" He held his breath, waiting for the bad news to be delivered. It wouldn't surprise him, but it would certainly deflate him. And it would be just about right for how his life had been going lately.

Sam chuckled and took a last drag off his cigarette. He got up and went to the window to flick it outside. His ass, high and firm, glowed in the moonlight, and Thad wondered if he would have to rethink his policy of not dating committed men. *Hell, with that ass, I may have to rethink my policy of being a total bottom.*

He's not talking because he's trying to think of the right way to tell me. Thad clutched a pillow to his chest, almost as if he were bracing himself for a blow, which he was.

Sam weighed down the bed as he slid back in beside him. "You silly boy. There's no one else. I said 'we' because I have a son. He came with me." Sam took Thad's face in his hands and snatched him up in his dark-eyed gaze. "There's no one else." He let go and Thad immediately missed the contact. "I travel light. I usually like, um, no complications? But when I saw you, I couldn't resist."

Before Thad could respond, Sam was on him again, kissing, tonguing, and finally pulling him onto his knees and mounting him from behind. Sam was no less tender and this time held out even longer before they both exploded, making enough noise that Thad worried about waking the neighbors.

It wasn't until they were falling asleep that the paranoid side of Thad caught up with him again, causing him to wonder if the fucking was a way to stave off further conversation. *Who is this son? Did Sam really just come to America for a change? How many people actually do that...or can even afford to? Stop it, now. He's here with me now...*

And they drifted off to sleep together, arms and legs intertwined, the room ripe with the smell of sweat and cum.

*

When Thad awakened, the morning's light, an invader, shone brightly into the room. He squinted and sat up in bed.

Alone.

Dream images scattered. All Thad could remember was fog, a full moon, woods, and the furry face of a black dog—wolf?—with a pointed snout. The animal turning to look at him. A splash of blood on a rock, looking black in the light from the moon... The dream images made him queasy, and he forced them from his mind.

Where was Sam? Thad cocked his head to listen. This was, after all, a studio. If Sam was still here, Thad could hear him. There would be the sound of a toilet flushing or water running. Otherwise, he'd see him, naked, in the morning light.

It was a vision Thad really wanted to have.

But he would be denied.

Then he heard something. A scratching at the bathroom door, like claws. *Scritch, scratch...*

He suddenly remembered Edith, forgotten and locked in the bathroom all night. A pang of guilt rushed through Thad. He glanced over at the clock next to the bed and saw it was almost ten. He couldn't remember when he had last slept so deeply and wakened so late.

I was really exhausted. He wanted to smile at the thought, but his elation at the memory of last night was muffled by the reality of this morning and waking up to Sam being gone. *He didn't even say goodbye...*

Wearily Thad swung his legs over the side of the bed. His ass felt sore, but it was a pleasant reminder of the night before. Edith must have realized he was stirring because her scratching grew more intense, accompanied by whining.

"I'm coming, stinker. Just hold on." He groped in his drawer for a pair of shorts and a T-shirt, dressed quickly, then slid into his flip-flops and grabbed the leash from its hook by the door.

Edith barely made it outside before letting go with a yellow torrent. Thad laughed. "I don't know where you keep all that." She looked up at him with her bulgy eyes, as if offended. "Sorry." He followed the dog down the street so she could find a suitable spot to complete her morning business.

It wasn't until Thad got back inside that he noticed the folded sheet of paper taped to the cover of his laptop. Dispirited, he quickly crossed over and snatched the paper from the computer's brushed chrome surface. *Do I really want to read this? How can I not read it? Besides, it might just say something like "Had a wonderful time; call you tonight."* But Thad was not enough of an optimist to put much stock in that.

He opened the note and began reading.

My Dear Thad,

Last night was wonderful. Amazing. You are the first person I met since I came to Seattle that I really want to know better.

But now I am afraid. Afraid of getting too attached. Afraid of involvements. I need to concentrate on my restaurant and my son. If you were just one of those one-night stands, I would not have bothered to write to you like this. But you are a special man. You already got my heart beating a little faster. I like that. And I don't like that because it takes me away from what I came here to do.

So, for now, maybe we should not see each other again. I hope you understand. Maybe when the restaurant gets on its feet, I can have someone like you in my life again. But right now, I think you're just too much temptation.

Thad sat down heavily on his bed, staring at the letter. All the jubilation, all the hope, all the lust deflated out of him like air out of a balloon. Had he done something wrong? The note was on the order of the old saw "It's not you; it's me," but he knew most of the time people just said that to bypass offending the dumped party. Thad, after losing his job and never having had much luck in the romance department, couldn't help but augment his lowered self-esteem with questions about his prowess in bed, his looks, the size of his manhood... Was he tight enough? Was he clean enough?

And maybe what Sam said about a son was true, but maybe he'd lied about there being no one else. If there was a son, there had to be a wife...or at least had to have been at one time. Or at the very least, someone he was with long enough to give her a son. Maybe she had been in the back last night, cooking his pastina? He pictured a dark-haired Sicilian woman, her chocolate-brown eyes peering out at him from the kitchen, her heart thumping with jealousy.

Save the creativity for my job hunt or my next job, if I ever find it...

Edith, always able to sense things beyond what a dog should rationally be capable of picking up on, made a mighty leap to join him on the bed. She lay down beside Thad so her little body pressed against his thigh, then put her head on his lap to stare up at him with sad eyes. The gesture brought a lump to Thad's throat and a hot stab of wet at the corners of his eyes.

Don't be stupid. He was just another guy. And they all have baggage. The only surprise is that maybe—for a few hours—I thought this one might be different.

Thad slumped back on the bed, one leg dangling over the edge. Edith shifted a bit but maintained her vigil, faithful as always.

Thad tried to comfort himself with the knowledge that Sam had at least tried to be kind in his note. And maybe what the man had said was true. Seattle was full of good restaurants of every stripe, and it must be hard to make a go of one, especially one with a popular lakefront location where the rent would be astronomical. Maybe, just maybe, he was so taken with Thad—as he had said—that he just couldn't afford the distraction of a hot redhead right now.

Sure. That's why he didn't even bother to wake me up to give me a kiss goodbye.

Thad sat back up and scratched Edith behind the ears. "The hunt continues, my dear. Both for an exciting man and a fulfilling job. Or maybe the other way around? Who knows if there is even any such thing out there?" He stood. "But for right now, you and I are not gonna think about flaky men, a silent job market, or anything depressing."

Thad forced himself to smile and pressed the palms of his hands against his eyes to halt the flow of any more tears. He took in a great quivering breath. "Right now, you and I are going to have a big breakfast. Some chicken for you and a big stack of pancakes for me. Buttermilk—with sausage." He picked Edith up and headed toward the kitchen area, where he set Edith on a barstool at the counter that divided the kitchen from the rest of the apartment. He glanced back at the dog, who looked for all the world like a patron at a bar, waiting for her martini to be served. "And after that, we're gonna head over to Discovery Park and take a nice, long hike. Maybe we'll even see a few seals on the beach. Sound good?"

Edith opened her mouth to pant. Thad could have sworn she was smiling.

Chapter Four

SEPTEMBER

All around him he sees roads going nowhere. Huge ramps and posts holding them up that lead toward the sky, as if aliens had built them for takeoff strips. They almost glow, grayish in the shimmering light of the full moon. Surrounding them are trees, grasses, growing wild in a riot around a lily-pad-flecked canal. The wind, cold this September night, rustles through the treetops, making a sound like whispering and sending the weakest of the leaves, harbingers of fall, down to the ground.

Even though he has dark-adapted eyes, it would be difficult to see were it not for the moon tonight, which is glorious, a pale-faced imitator of the sun. A veil of silver cloaks everything here in the Washington Park Arboretum. Night has become a kind of day, one that exists in black and white. The pale light and the ability to actually see along the path has brought out many wanderers in the woods. They—all of them men, all of them solitary—make restless circuits of the trails going through the woods and along the canal. They stop here and there, where a bent tree or a copse of bushes provides a kind of shelter, looking for another soul who will elevate them from their loneliness for a few minutes. Some have succeeded—condom wrappers and condoms themselves, used, litter the ground, and some even hang from branches.

He also hunts...but not for the same thing. While they search for the warmth of sexual connection, hungry for the taste of cum, he looks for the coldness of destruction and the taste of blood. He lifts his snout to test the cool air and is rewarded with the smell of at least a dozen men, traversing the trails that cut through the woods of the park. He has slipped through the shadows, watching as the men exchange silent signals with one another, couple, then separate to wander back to the parking lot. Some of them hurry with their heads hung low, as if ashamed of what they have done. Others, shameless, walk jauntily back to their cars or their homes in the neighborhoods bordering the park, satisfied with their release.

Disgusting.

The creature pads along a trail, waiting for one of the men to break free of the others, to follow a trail perhaps down to the canal's edge, to separate from the pack. It is the ones who stay by themselves, perhaps the ones too fearful to actually do what they came here for, that he wants. Vulnerable. Alone.

He is quick and sure when he attacks. There will be no screams to alert the others. There won't even be a scuffle. There will be only death and feasting, silent and sure, gliding in on one of these men, unsuspecting, like a shadow. The element of surprise has always been his trump and his calling card. His stealth and razor-sharp fangs will ensure a quick demise, painful for only a second or two, until blood and flesh is rendered and offered up to him like a gift.

He revels in the anticipation of the kill. He will satisfy his own ferocious hunger, in his belly for certain, but also for the elusive taste of justice. These men deserve to have something bad happen to them. Look at them! In a public place, looking to sate their perverted desires, to connect with strangers in a way that should be reserved for private, for time alone with a creature one loves and bears some commitment to...

He is an old-fashioned monster. He feels no remorse for what he is about to do. In its own way, he knows that his hunting and killing is for the common good, eradicating those who foul the world with heedless desire and warped attractions.

He pads along a trail and hops jauntily along the wooden surface of a small bridge, making not a sound. Ahead, one has separated far enough from the pack that the beast thinks he may have a chance, especially if the man is foolish enough to duck into a cluster of foliage that will shield dark couplings from passersby as close as a few feet away. He knows his alfresco meal will be over within seconds. It's not the length of the meal that defines its quality.

From a few feet away, he pants, licking his chops, and watches the man. He is tall, clad in a pair of tight-fitting jeans, boots, and a dark T-shirt, much too lightweight for this chilly night but perfect for showing off biceps that have been pumped unnaturally large and a chest that spans superhero width. The creature is certain that such physical dimensions make the man a desirable candidate, a kind of trophy or reward. But his bulging muscles and cocky walk are all for show. He knows there is no strength to back them up. He will be just as easy to bring down as all the rest. And like all the rest, he will not even make a sound.

He will go for the neck first.

He trots along on his paws, heart rate increasing, his salivary glands working so hard that a line of drool drips from his mouth to glisten silver on the ground, like the trail of a slug. Embarrassed, he notes that he also has an erection and wishes it would go away. This isn't about sex. It's about food. And justice.

The man does as he predicts: ducks into a kind of makeshift shelter of leaves and branches...and waits. Perhaps in the past, this protocol has been successful. He senses a confidence coming from the man as he loiters in the darkness, rubbing his crotch and waiting for someone to come along and drop to his knees before him to worship. Or to bend over in a sick display of surrender.

But tonight the man's fantasies will not be fulfilled. The beast enters the little cave of trees, and the man stiffens when he sees him. His mouth drops open. He steps back and turns to run, stumbling through briars and tree trunks. He falls.

And the monster is upon him, going, as planned, for the throat first and ripping it open so the only sound that comes out is a slight gurgling. Contrary to what he thought, the man is strong, batting and punching at him even as the life ebbs out of him in scarlet spurts from his throat. The creature wants to yelp. These death-throe blows are brutal. They hurt. Just like any other natural animal, he experiences pain. The hurt heightens his rage, and his powerful jaws clamp down on the man's face, his chest, the softer flesh of his belly, and finally through the denim and onto his cock, ripping it from the man's body.

A red haze rises up as the monster feeds, shredding the body until it is hardly even recognizable as a human being. The sharp metallic tang of blood hangs in the air, feeding his hunger and making him want more.

He feeds far longer than usual, eating parts he would normally leave behind. But he is lost in a frenzy. So lost he does not hear the voices behind him right away. But when a scream pierces the darkness, the creature looks back to observe a trio of humans watching the carnage, stunned quiet by terror and awe.

He has an urge to go after them but has enough presence of mind to know this would be dangerously foolhardy. Instead he turns, tail between his legs, to dash through the brush. He knows he is so fast, he will be nothing but a black/gray blur. Knows that, later, these witnesses may even question what their eyes showed them.

Chapter Five

Thad awakened with the same feeling of anticipation as so many other days this past month, quickly quashed by loss. He sat up, rubbing the sleep from his eyes, and wondered if there would ever come a time when he would awaken and *not* think about Sam. He turned to look out the east-facing window to the sky, tinged with pink at the horizon, the trees and houses nearby silhouettes in the relentless creeping in of day. He sighed, glancing down at Edith, who still slept, curled into a tight ball at the foot of his bed.

He wondered, for about the thirtieth time, how it could be that he was *still* waking up with Sam on his mind. For crying out loud, it had been only a one-night stand. Lord knew Thad had had plenty of those, and none of those men hung around like a traumatic memory, to poke and prod him upon waking each morning. Those previous one-nighters had been forgotten as quickly as dreams. More than once Thad had encountered one a few weeks later on the street and barely recognized him.

So why had this Sam character gotten so under his skin? Sure, he was hot, one of the hottest men Thad had ever been with. Porn-star hot. And he seemed kind, to boot. And he could cook. Thad had to concede those were pretty good reasons for being unforgettable.

Yet Sam had rejected him. That alone seemed good enough reason to put the man behind him, and not in a good way.

This past month Thad had avoided passing in front of the Blue Moon Café, even if it meant abandoning his much-loved runs around the circumference of Green Lake. Now he would take a more urban path westward into the U District, or head over to Ravenna Park, where he could run along wooded trails. He knew it was silly, avoiding the beauty of the lake, with its still blue water, views of the Cascades, and even, sometimes, Mount Rainier, just to sidestep passing a restaurant.

But he couldn't help himself. He was still sore from the magic of that night. Not physically, of course, but emotionally. It felt like someone had placed magic in his hands and then ripped it away. He wondered if he would ever stop longing for the magic.

He had tried to blot out Sam's influence on his life with the usual weakling's remedies: vodka and cheap sex. He had spent more nights and more money he didn't really have at various Capitol Hill gay bars, searching for that one perfect drink, that one perfect man who would obliterate Sam from his memory. But all the vodka did was dull his senses and give him a headache the next day that made him useless. And he was never able to bring himself to find an answer to "my place or yours" with any response other than the age-old chestnut, "I have to get up early in the morning."

He left offers on the table that he would have—pre-Sam—snatched up with hot-blooded gratitude. He didn't know what was wrong with him.

Yes, he did.

Sam.

The hell with Sam, he thought, not really believing himself, and hoisted himself from a bed he would have preferred to spend the entire day in, feeling sorry for himself. He padded to the bathroom, where he pissed, and splashed water on his face. In the mirror he looked for signs of distress: rings under his eyes, paleness, a general slacking downward of his lips, and found nothing. At least his despair had not yet caught up with his youthful good looks! Small consolation, especially when those looks were squandered with too many lonely nights at home, pining for a man who clearly did not want him.

Enough of this! Thad returned to the studio proper, where Edith had been roused by his movements and was now on the bed, wriggling around on her back, scratching. When she spied Thad out of the corner of her eye, she flipped over, bounded out of bed, and went to sit and wait by the door.

"Okay, okay. Just hold on...or hold *it*." Thad hurried to dress in a pair of old jeans, University of Washington sweatshirt, and his Asics. The mornings of late had been chilly, and Thad damned himself by wishing for someone to snuggle up against to keep him warm. But not just anyone...

Enough of this! Thad grabbed the leash from its hook by the door and stooped to attach it to Edith's harness. Today would be different. Today he and Edith would not only go for a leisurely walk around the neighborhood, they would also stop for coffee at the little café on Latona. They would enjoy the scenery. They would race each other to the top of a hill.

They would not think about Sam.

And today Thad had employment of a sort to look forward to. Not paying, of course. That would have been too much to ask for. But at least he could feel he was doing something good in the world, something with purpose. Today Thad would begin a weekly volunteer shift at

Lifelong AIDS Alliance, which provided food and all sorts of assistance to people living with AIDS and HIV. Thad figured, with all the free time on his hands, the least he could do was use some of it to give back to his community. And it was not lost on him that only by the grace of God was he not a beneficiary himself of LLA's services.

And although he wouldn't admit this to anyone but himself—and maybe Edith—he thought such an organization would be chock full of homosexual men, one of whom might just have the ability to erase Sam from his mind.

There I go again, thinking about Sam. Cut it out!

Thad stopped to watch Edith as she sniffed at a fire hydrant—he called this practice "reading her p-mail"—and forced himself to think of the day ahead and what it might bring.

*

Thad's volunteer shift was in LLA's warehouse, packing bags of food for weekly delivery to clients. The warehouse also housed the kitchen, which cooked hot meals for people in need.

He was only a little nervous as he found a parking space in LLA's lot and went in its front doors for the first time since his volunteer orientation meeting.

The warehouse was tight, with a couple of long tables for assembling the bags of food that included a week's worth of staples. It had high ceilings and rows of shelving, upon which sat stacked boxes and boxes of almost every sort of packaged food imaginable. Two huge industrial-sized refrigerators held stuff like dairy, produce, and meat. The kitchen was busy too, with the voices of the cooks carrying over into the warehouse workspace, and the smell of onions, peppers, and garlic made Thad's mouth water. This week Thad would be helping two other volunteers fill bags with red beans, rice, lettuce, milk, juice, two different kinds of canned vegetables, ground turkey, and for fun, bags of M&M's. A local bakery had also donated loaves of fresh sourdough bread.

The guy who ran the warehouse, a fellow 'mo in cool glasses and a fondness for horror movies and professional wrestlers, kept the energy level high by blasting out eighties disco music. Thad's coworkers, alas, were not the handsome gay men he had hoped for, but a University of Washington coed, who was doing volunteer service for class credit in one of her social work classes, and a young man, very quiet, who was volunteering as part of court-ordered community service. The guy barely looked up from his work, and if he weren't crafted from flesh, muscle, and bone, would have most likely been invisible.

The work quickly became assembly line, in spite of the efforts of Madonna, Donna Summer, Prince, Morris Day and the Time, and Anita Ward to create a party-like atmosphere. And even though Thad mentally patted himself on the back for doing this charitable work, he found himself glancing down surreptitiously at his watch to see how much longer until the end of his shift. The passage of time had slowed to a crawl, because every time he looked down at the analog face, he expected to see a half hour or forty-five minutes, but the watch only mocked him with a movement of five minutes.

Perhaps he radiated his boredom, because eventually a very cute guy came back into the warehouse from the front and appeared to be looking for someone. Thad took him in: blond hair, blue eyes, a few wisps of hair on his chin, baggy jeans, and a black T-shirt with the word

"Buzzkill" emblazoned in white block letters across the front. A tattooed tribal ring poked out from the bottom of one of his sleeves.

He was anything but a buzzkill. Perhaps the T-shirt should read "Welcome Distraction." The guy wasn't Thad's usual type. He normally liked beefy, bearded men, but Thad wouldn't travel *that* road. Actually, it was a relief to be drawn to someone nothing like Sam, someone whose looks were Nordic rather than Mediterranean, with a lanky build instead of burly. It also helped that the man was a decade or two younger than Sam, and thus closer to Thad's own age.

So Thad caught the guy's gaze and gave him a smile. He had no idea what the blond was doing in the warehouse or if he would even smile back. But he not only rewarded Thad with a brilliant—and sexy—lopsided grin in return, the guy marched right up to him, extending his hand.

"Hi, I'm Jared."

Thad took his hand and probably shook it for longer than he should have, staring into Jared's eyes and grinning stupidly. Fortunately his flirtatious handshake seemed welcome.

"Thad. Are you here to volunteer?" There was more than a little hope in how Thad phrased his question.

"Nah. I already volunteer at the front desk. But they sent me back here to see if we could grab one of you guys to come up front and help out making some calls to local stores and restaurants for donations." Jared stepped back and made a little twirling motion with his finger. "Turn around."

Puzzled, Thad did as he was told.

Jared smiled. "You'll do. You wanna come up and give us a hand for an hour or two? I already cleared it with Steve." Steve was the warehouse manager.

"Sure. I could use a break from this." As they were heading toward the front office area of the charity, Thad had to ask, "Why did you need me to turn around for you? How does that have anything to do with making phone calls?"

"It doesn't. That was for my personal benefit." Jared laughed, and Thad smiled because the laugh was so warm.

For the first time in a month, Thad's thoughts drifted far from Sam.

Jared took Thad to an empty cubicle and told him to sit. He leaned over Thad as he arranged a ream of papers for him. Thad couldn't help but notice how this maneuver placed Jared's crotch in close proximity to his face. *Behave! I'm doing charity work here!* But Jared's nearness made it very hard to concentrate on what the guy said. If he wanted to do this job right, though—and really help—he needed to listen. He forced himself to stare at a poster on the opposite wall about free HIV testing at a local bathhouse.

"So this is our list of restaurants, grocery stores, and produce markets. We get a lot of donations, but with requests coming in all the time, we always need more. I went through and highlighted the ones we haven't dealt with before for you to call."

Thad looked up into Jared's blue eyes and tried to smile but already could feel a little animal gnawing inside his stomach. "So it's sort of like telemarketing?" Thad was not the most outgoing person in the world, which was probably why he had been drawn to a career like writing, which gave him a measure of solitude in his working life.

Jared laughed. "I suppose you could say that. But here's the thing. Most of these people won't mind hearing from you, unlike they would if someone was calling about their Discover Card or whatever. You know, it's a good thing you're doing. Even if they don't deep down want to be bothered, they'll at least be nice to you."

"That's reassuring." Thad looked down at the list. "What do I say?"

"Easy." Jared pulled a sheet from a drawer. "You have a script. Now, I am not saying repeat it word for word. In fact, I advise against it—you don't want to sound canned. But just kind of stick to the general idea: who you are, who LLA is, what you're calling about, and how they can help. It's not too tough. After you get someone to volunteer goods, just jot it down in the log here." Jared flipped open a red notebook already partially filled with donors. "Okay? You ready?"

Thad nodded, looking over the script.

"I'll be right over at the front desk if you need anything."

"How about if I need a martini?"

Jared snorted. "That could be arranged. But *after* the shift." He winked at Thad and walked away.

Thad felt, suddenly, a renewed sense of confidence and very little of the trepidation he'd experienced as Jared laid out his task for him. He placed his finger on the first highlighted number on the list and began dialing.

Jared was right. Most of the people were very receptive to his call. And after Thad made a few calls, several of them successful, he no longer felt nervous about what he was doing.

Until he got to the third page of numbers.

The notation and number stopped him cold. His heart began to thud uncomfortably in his chest. His palms slicked with sweat. *Oh no. I can't call this one.* Thad looked and saw there were only a few highlighted numbers remaining. Maybe he could just skip over this one and come back to it. Maybe he would run out of time before he got to it.

That's no way to think. That's not what I came here to do. I came to help. Now just put my fingers on the phone buttons and call. I may not even have to talk to him.

Thad sighed and looked at the name on the list again. The Blue Moon Café. What if Sam answered?

So what if he does? I spent one night with him a month ago. Do I really think he'll remember my voice? I could use any name. Like, I don't know, Jared Holmes. Thad chuckled at the thought. *Besides, Sam may not even answer the phone. Just get it over with.*

Thad picked up the receiver and cradled it between his ear and shoulder as he punched in the numbers. *Be busy. Give me a machine. Ring endlessly.* Prayers ran through his mind even as he knew, with a certainty as sure as he knew his hair was red and he grew up in Chicago, that Sam would pick up the phone.

"Blue Moon Café. Sam speaking. What can I do for you today?"

You can take back that stupid message you left taped to my computer. You can call me again. You can say you're sorry. You can fuck me again within an inch of my life. Thad clamped a hand to his mouth to stifle a completely inappropriate giggle. He sucked in some air and thought he'd better start talking before Sam hung up.

The words that issued forth weren't drawn from the script in front of him. They were a complete surprise...even to Thad. His heart ached too much, and this sudden, surprise encounter with Sam caught him completely off guard.

"Sam? It's Thad. You remember me? We met about a month ago at your restaurant." Thad lowered his voice and hunched into the phone so his voice would not carry over the cubicle wall. "You came back to my place and spent the night."

The words poured out without thought, guided by hunger and the pent-up pain of rejection. Thad knew he had no business having this conversation—at least not right now—but he couldn't help himself. He realized he should have had the courage to make this call long ago.

Sam didn't say anything for a while, long enough for Thad to fear he would hang up. But finally he spoke, and his voice came out even, deep, and mellow. "Of course I remember you." He paused again, and Thad imagined he was considering what he would say next. "There has not been a day when I haven't thought about you...and about our night together."

"Really?" Thad assumed all along that Sam had simply used him and brushed him off. To ease the hurt, he had worked this past month to convince himself that Sam had simply wanted a piece of ass and Thad had been convenient that September night.

"Yes, really." Sam sighed, and in the exhalation, Thad could hear—really hear—the man's regret. And it made Thad smile, but not in a vicious way. A little flame of hope brightened in his belly. "I have picked up the phone a dozen times to call you, to say I was sorry. But then things happened..." Sam paused for a long time, long enough for

Thad to wonder what kinds of things; there was such dark import attached to Sam's simple phrase. "And I never got around to it. Or I thought better of dragging you into my crazy life."

"I wish you'd let me decide if I want to be dragged or not."

Sam blew out some air. "You're right."

"I am?"

Sam laughed. "Yes. You are a grown man...and a very fine one too. I should have let you make up your own mind about me. Is it too late? Can we try once more?"

"Are you playing with me?"

"No, but I'd like to be."

Thad closed his eyes, leaned back, and laughed out loud. He had gone from fear to joy in five minutes or less. But there was still a small voice in him that remained cautious, the voice of self-protection, maybe. Thad scratched his head and debated whether he should ask the question on his mind, but in the end decided this was one of those now or never moments. If he didn't ask, he would always wonder, and that would cloud any hope he had for a future with Sam. "Um, this all sounds great. And the answer to 'Can we try again?' is, of course, yes. But Sam, I have to wonder, why the change of heart? You were pretty emphatic in your little note that you didn't think this was the right time."

"I know, I know. And to be honest with you, it's still not the right time. But sometimes, in matters of the heart, it doesn't always make sense to be so practical. Maybe if I hadn't heard your voice again, I could have, how do you say it over here, stuck to my guns? But when I heard you, I knew I had to see you again."

"But why?"

"Because you are a gorgeous and caring man. Because we fit together. What do you mean, why?" Sam sniffed as if outraged.

Thad laughed. He felt a bit light-headed. This was the last thing he'd expected as a result of volunteering today. He leaned back, drinking in the warm, deep timbre of Sam's voice as he spoke.

"I don't know, Thad. My life... It is complicated. There are dark sides and light sides. You don't know. You just don't know."

Thad paused for a minute, trying to figure out what the man was talking about. In the end, his hope and eagerness to see Sam again made him gloss over his last statement, attributing it, quite reasonably, to the demands and problems everyone experienced, like not finding enough hours in the day to do everything one wanted. That's what Sam meant, wasn't it? "Oh, I think I know."

Sam chuckled, but there was little mirth in it. "I doubt that you do." He took a breath, and Thad could feel Sam's mood changing through the phone. His tone was suddenly lighter. "But, to use another American expression, we cross those bridges when we come to them, yes?"

"Sounds like a good plan."

They stopped talking for a few seconds, and then Sam said, "I want you to meet *mia famiglia*. They all come here with me from Sicily. If we are going to make a good start, especially with Italians, you have to start with the family. We are closed tomorrow night, but I want you to come for dinner. Can you?"

Thad thought, for approximately three seconds, about being coy and saying something like "Let me check my calendar" but knew he would be kidding no one but himself. "Yes! Of course! What time?"

"Eight o'clock...at the restaurant."

"Can I bring anything?"

"Like what? Food? You're asking *me* if you can bring food?" Sam laughed so heartily and so loud, Thad held the receiver away from his ear.

"Right."

"See you tomorrow, then?"

"I can't wait."

Thad hung up. It wasn't until several minutes later that he realized he had never asked Sam for a donation from the café. Oh well, he would be seeing him the next night. The next night! He could ask him then.

Thad drifted off, imagining the evening, painting himself in a favorable and irresistible light, seeing Sam's Italian family's face glowing with approval and instant acceptance. He would charm them, make them laugh, make them see how he could easily be one of them. *Slow down there, skipper. I'm getting a tad ahead of myself here.* He also let his mind wander to a time after the plates had been cleared and thought that, even if he didn't bring anything, he could certainly provide a tasty dessert for Sam.

"You look like you're about a thousand miles away. What *are* you thinking about?"

Thad nearly lurched out of his seat at the sound of the voice behind him. He turned to see Jared looking down at him and grinning. Thad felt his face redden, almost as if he had been caught with his hand down his pants, which would have been the next step if his thoughts about dessert and Sam had continued in the same vein. "Nothing!"

Jared laughed. "If you say so. Anyway, we're finishing up here. I just wanted to see if you were still up for that drink. There's a place right around the corner that makes a wicked dirty martini."

Thad felt at a loss. Here was Jared, looking all hopeful, as he had every reason to be. But now Thad was simply not that interested in the admittedly good-looking blond. Maybe he should have been. But the phone call to Sam erased all thoughts of other men right out of his head.

But he couldn't just renege on the offer. He had led Jared to think earlier that he was interested. He would have to, pardon the expression, set Jared straight. And having a drink with him would give Thad the chance to wax rhapsodic on Sam and to let Jared know there was no hope for them to be anything more than friends. But one could never have too many of those, Thad told himself. So even though he really just wanted to go home and fantasize more about tomorrow night's prospects, he forced himself to smile and say, "That sounds perfect."

The bar, a tiny, dark place called Mangroves, was literally right around the corner. It had a few tables— maybe a half-dozen—scattered around the room. A massive old-school oak bar with a line of padded black-and-chrome stools in front of it sat along one wall. A large mirror hung behind the bar, and above that a row of tiny white lights that seemed to provide the only illumination for the room.

A happy-hour crowd had pretty well filled the place to capacity, and the sounds of dozens of conversations, with a Beyoncé sound track, made the place seem lively. Jared grabbed Thad's arm as they entered and leaned close to talk in his ear. "See that table over there in the corner? Those guys are just getting ready to leave. Why don't you grab it before it's gone? I'll go get the first round."

And Jared was off toward the bar, leaving Thad to claim the table. He sat down just before two older heavyset gentlemen were about to take it. "Sorry!" he said brightly.

"Ah...the younger and the prettier," one of the older men sighed. "They get everything." The pair wandered away.

Thad settled in and thought about what he was doing. Was he leading Jared on?

No, I am not being a tease or leading anyone on. This is just a drink with a friend. He has no reason to expect anything more.

Thad knew his thinking was all very reasonable until he factored in the electricity that had passed between him and Jared earlier that day.

Ah well, life is never easy or uncomplicated, is it?

Thad didn't have the chance to ruminate further on things since Jared, with a smile and a flourish, set a paper napkin and a chilled martini glass before him. Thad was pleased to see the liquid inside was cloudy—very dirty—and the bar had added the luxury of bleu-cheese-stuffed olives.

"This looks perfect. Thank you." Thad took a tiny sip, since the glass was almost filled to overflowing, and set it back down, letting the ice-cold vodka trickle down his throat.

Jared sat across from him with a mug of draft beer. "You can have it, buddy. I'll stick with my Mac & Jack's." He raised his mug to Thad and gave him a smile that had probably broken a thousand hearts, lopsided and undeniably sexy.

The two talked for the better part of an hour, with Thad trying, without much luck, to insert Sam into the conversation. He couldn't really say he had a boyfriend because that was not technically quite true, at least not yet, and the opportunities for saying something about how excited he was to be getting together with this new, hot guy just seemed rude. However, he did ignore the pressure of Jared's foot on his calf until Jared gave up and moved it away. Thad was also careful not to let his gaze linger too long.

After they finished their second drink, Jared abruptly asked, "So, Thad, what are your plans for tonight?" Jared cocked his head and fixed him with the grin that, even though Thad felt he only had eyes for Sam, was still tempting.

Thad knew where this was going. And another Thad, the pre-Sam Thad, would have followed right along, doing things that would make his mama hang her head in shame. But now the prospect of something more physical with Jared simply made him uncomfortable, as if he would be cheating. But he wasn't quick enough to come up with anything other than "Not much. You?"

"Well..." Jared took a deep breath and increased the wattage on his killer smile. "I was hoping I might lure this hot redhead I met today back to my place." He smiled. "He seems like the type who could take whatever I dish out." Jared chuckled. "I live just up the hill, near Volunteer Park." He put his hand over Thad's. "We could be there in five minutes."

Thad grinned politely. And pulled his hand back to let it rest in his lap. The gesture wiped the smile right from Jared's face.

"What's the matter, Thad? Afraid that animal will eat you up?"

Thad cocked his head. "Huh? No, I... I just don't think it's a good idea. I... I'm kind of seeing someone, you know?"

Jared shook his head. "Just my luck. All the good ones are taken." He shrugged and sat back in his chair, splaying his legs in front of him, more visibly relaxed, it seemed, now that the moment had passed. Thad was glad—and liked Jared better—that the guy didn't make a big deal out of being turned down. Maybe they *could* be friends, and if things went south with Sam again, maybe more.

But something Jared said had caused a tiny shiver to go through him. "What did you mean, was I afraid of some animal?"

Jared looked at him and cocked his head. "You mean you haven't heard about the latest killing?"

Now Thad really got a chill, one that coursed up and down his spine. He flashed back to the summer, when he had read about the man on Capitol Hill—where they were right now—who had been ripped to pieces in an alley. He had forgotten it until this very moment. "No. I haven't looked much at the news lately."

"Yeah." Jared leaned closer, and his eyes got bigger. "Some guy down at the Washington Park Arboretum got killed last night. It was just like that murder last month, with the poor dude being torn up and partially eaten." Jared shivered. "It's the second time a gay man has been killed in a known gay area. They're beginning to wonder if there's a connection, although it seems like both of these killings could have been done by an animal, last night especially. But here on the Hill? With all these people constantly around?" Jared hugged himself, like he was suddenly cold. "I doubt it. I just don't see how an animal who could do that kind of damage could roam around a busy neighborhood like Capitol Hill and not get noticed. No, I think this is the work of a major psycho." He let himself relax. "Anyway, I just wanted to be sure you weren't afraid of me because of that. Because really, hon, I'm a sheep in wolf's clothing."

"I'm sure. But I didn't even know about this second murder. You said this happened at the Arboretum?"

"Yeah. You know how cruisy that place is. There were a couple guys who saw a little of what happened, but I guess none of them was able to come up with a description other than a 'black blur.' Creepy, huh?"

"Very."

Thad glanced down at his watch. Edith would be waiting at home to go outside and to have her supper. "Listen, Jared. This has been really fun. And if it weren't for Sam, I would go home with you in a heartbeat. I'll probably kick myself anyway for not taking you up on your offer. But I need to get home to my dog."

"Oh? What kind?"

"A Chihuahua."

Jared smirked.

"No comments, please." Thad laughed. Could he have chosen a gayer breed? "Anyway, I hope we can do this again. Or maybe dinner sometime...or a movie?"

"Just not as a date, right?"

Thad shook his head. "I'm sorry, buddy, but I just need to see where things go with this new guy."

"He must be awfully hot to make you pass up a chance at this..." Jared gestured to his body, then laughed.

Thad liked him. And if he didn't want to further complicate his life, he knew he really should get going. So he stood and said goodbye, giving Jared a quick peck on the lips. "See you soon, okay?"

"Sure."

Thad hurried from the bar. Edith waited. And tomorrow Sam would be waiting.

Thad couldn't wait.

Chapter Six

Thad hadn't realized, when he'd visited the Blue Moon Café for the first time, that there was a small apartment in the back. Sam led him through the closed restaurant, which seemed kind of lonely and abandoned in the dark, with its empty tables stacked with upside-down chairs. An echo of conversation hung in the air, yet the place seemed unnaturally quiet, as if it were waiting for patrons to return and resume their conversations where they left off.

Before they headed through the kitchen, Sam turned to him, and his chocolate-eyed gaze drank in Thad. "I am so happy you came. I don't know if what I'm doing is right, but my heart says it doesn't matter."

His words made Thad tingle. Quickly Sam grabbed him and kissed him. What started out as a lighthearted peck of welcome quickly morphed into a full-blown, openmouthed, tongues-dueling lip-lock of unbridled passion. After what seemed like more than a couple of minutes had passed, Sam pulled away.

They both gasped and then laughed softly, hugging each other. Thad whispered, "You have such animal magnetism, Sam. I can't stand it." And he couldn't. He wanted to throw propriety—and dinner—to the wind and just drag the man back to his apartment, where maybe something could be done about this stiffness in his pants that felt on the verge of exploding.

But real life didn't work that way. So Thad gulped in some air, tried to think of anything other than Sam spreading himself out on top of him like some big furred beast, and said, "I'm really looking forward to meeting your family."

"And they you. And don't worry...we will get some time alone later."

"I'll hold you to that."

Sam led him through the door to the family apartment, and Thad got ambushed. He couldn't remember a time when he had been greeted so warmly and enthusiastically, especially by complete strangers. With no shyness, they grabbed him and hugged him, planting kisses on both cheeks. There was lots of murmuring in Italian that Thad didn't understand beyond "*ciao*" and "*prego*." Then Sam cut through the clutter and pulled Thad away from the mob of people.

"Slow down, everyone! Thad is going to be frightened away by all of you. In America they are not so forward. Let me introduce you one at a time."

Sam reached out to an old woman, small but with a dignified bearing. She had perfectly white hair, cut short and combed back away from a face Thad thought was still beautiful, stunning in its grace and warmth. He could imagine what a knockout she must have been when she was in her twenties. She wore a simple rust-colored pantsuit and gold jewelry. Her large brown eyes took him in, and she smiled. Sam didn't need to say, "My mama. Sarah." Once more Thad found himself enveloped in a hug and lips planted on each cheek. She pulled back to hold his hands and stare up at him as if she were deciding if he passed muster. She looked at Sam and nodded, then said something in Italian that made the others laugh. "She says you are a good one."

Thad nodded at the woman and said, "Grazie."

"My mama doesn't speak English too good yet, but she will." A young woman with long dark hair stepped forward. She had a large nose and stunning olive eyes framed in long black lashes and wore a simple black dress with a strand of what appeared to Thad's untrained eyes to be real pearls. Tottering on spike heels, she said, "I'm Graziela," and extended her hand. Her fingers were long, topped with manicured bloodred nails. They shook hands. "I'm very pleased to meet you."

"And I you." Thad looked to Sam for further clarification. Was this the wife he'd worried about? A butterfly ascended in his stomach. What sort of night was he in for? He realized he didn't really know Sam at all, physical attraction and lust aside.

Sam said, "This is my baby sister. She's a beauty, no?"

"Oh yes!" Thad smiled broadly and pulled Graziela toward him to hug her. "I'm so happy you're Sam's sister!" *God, I sound like an idiot!* "I mean, I'm really pleased to meet Sam's sister, er, you, Graziela."

Sam smirked at him, giving a little shake of his head. "And this is Giovanni, my brother." Giovanni's presence had barely registered on Thad's overwhelmed brain when the man stepped forward to shake his hand. But when he came forward now, Thad took notice. He was, paradoxically, very similar to Sam, yet very unlike him. Where Sam was broad, bearish, and muscular, Giovanni was tall and thin. The writer in Thad conjured up words like "regal" and "imperial." Giovanni's bearing was elegant, aided by the cut of the simple black silk suit he wore. Unlike Sam, he didn't sport a beard, but Thad could tell he was just as hirsute. Thick black stubble covered his face. He had the same penetrating dark-brown eyes as his brother.

"It's really good to meet you, Thad. Sam has told me a lot about you. Welcome to our home." Giovanni's English was perfect, with scarcely the trace of an accent.

Sam explained, "Giovanni came over here before the rest of us. And he spent some time in the States in his twenties also. But it was Giovanni who came first to set things up for the rest of us, after Papa was killed..."

Thad looked over at Sam in surprise. He caught a glimmer of what he could only describe as rage pass through Sam's eyes. The group was quiet for only a second before Graziela chimed in. "Before Papa's *accident*, you mean, Sam." She gave him a pointed stare.

"Sure." Sam glanced down at the floor. It was obvious this discussion was closed. But Thad knew there was a lot more to the story than was being said.

There was a moment of uncomfortable silence, and then Sam made Thad jump by yelling toward the hallway leading off from the living room. "Hey, Domenic! You gonna come out here and meet our guest?"

Thad expected a little boy to emerge from the back of the apartment and was stunned when Domenic came out. He remembered him immediately. He was the drop-dead gorgeous bartender he had noticed on his first visit to the Blue Moon Café last month.

So this was his son? How old was Sam anyway?

Domenic came toward him, not smiling. Under different circumstances, Thad would have found the man's gruff, surly countenance sexy, but tonight he would have welcomed a smile. He tried to elicit one from Domenic by giving him his own broad grin.

Domenic wore all black, which suited his shaved head and heavy stubble. The shirt was tight enough to reveal the powerful network of muscles lurking beneath. The word "sleek" popped into Thad's mind. Domenic held out his hand and, when Thad took it, grasped it hard enough to hurt. "So you are Papa's new boyfriend? Pleased to meet you."

Thad raised an eyebrow to Sam and returned his gaze to Domenic. "Me too. I hope we can be friends." The insecure part of Thad couldn't help but wonder if Domenic's greeting was tinged with sarcasm.

"For fun, we call him Demonic."

Domenic simply shook his head, not smiling, as he gave his father a look that said *Don't even try*. What he said in actuality was, "That's right. So you should watch your step, buddy." He gave Thad a playful—or at least Thad hoped it was playful—poke in the chest.

Dinner was beyond Thad's wildest imaginings, in culinary terms. He knew it would be good, but the food weighing down the table that night was transporting. The tastes and smells went beyond anything Thad had experienced before. He had grown up on classic American comfort food like meat loaf, macaroni and cheese, and canned vegetables.

They started with an antipasto of small artichokes stuffed with breadcrumbs and Parmigiano-Reggiano and drizzled with fruity olive oil. For the pasta course, there was orecchiette pasta aioli flaked with red pepper, and then veal, lightly breaded and cooked in wine and lemon juice.

"You eat like this every night?" Thad asked near the end of the meal, when he felt as if he needed to unbutton the top button of his jeans and was delirious at being stuffed with some of the best food he had ever eaten.

Graziela laughed. "Not every night. We like to show off for our guests. When it's just us, we probably not gonna do all the courses. We are simple people. And we like simple stuff like greens and beans, wedding soup with a good piece of bread, or maybe a roasted chicken."

Sam piped in. "Of course, we often bring home what's left from the restaurant and make a meal from that...or we eat while we're working, usually the special."

As Thad tried to eat—he had to be polite, after all—the gorgonzola, provolone, grapes, tangerines, and walnuts in their shells that had been laid out for dessert, he was glad he didn't have to say much during the meal. Thad had always considered himself a bit of an introvert, and with this group, it would have been hard to compete. But the chatter at the table was nearly unceasing, much of it centering around the new restaurant, stories from the old country, and childhood reminiscences of the siblings. A good quarter of the discussion was in Italian, and Thad knew they didn't even realize they were slipping into the native tongue until they looked at him, sheepish, and translated. He didn't mind. He felt like part of the family.

After espresso accompanied by a small grappa, Sam announced to the group that it was time to walk Thad home.

"What? And leave the women, I guess, to clean up the mess? Things were supposed to be different in America!" Graziela yelled. Thad was afraid she was really furious until she began laughing. She shook her head, "Go on, brother, you see your friend safely home. I'll save some cleanup for you."

Thad made his good nights, thanking everyone—especially Sam's mother, Sarah—profusely and reminding them that he hoped to see them again soon. "But one thing I can promise," he said with a smile, "is that I would *never* dare cook for you."

They thought that was funny. Giovanni told him they actually liked Hamburger Helper and iceberg lettuce once in a while. Thad realized he was trying to be friendly and rib him, but he wasn't so sure he was flattered by the assumption.

Outside, the night air had taken a real turn for the cold. Thad moved close to Sam and grabbed one of his arms, pulling it around him like a stole. Sam stiffened for only a moment, then left his arm where Thad had put it. "In my country, a man putting his arm around another man like a lover would never go over, unless, of course, the men were drunk."

"Well, I am drunk!" Thad said. "Drunk on love." He felt a burning blush immediately rise to his cheeks. It was way too soon to be saying such things. He hastened to lighten the mood. "God! I am so stuffed, I think I need to purge."

Sam laid a gentle kiss on his cheek. "I don't care who sees us. In Seattle, things are, how do you say it? Um, more laid-back?"

"Yeah, but I wouldn't go overboard yet."

Back at Thad's apartment, Thad hurried to take out Edith. As she sidled by Sam, as if she didn't want to touch him or even get close to him, she snapped at him. It looked like the dog really had every intention of wounding the guy, and Sam sprang back, just out of reach of the Chihuahua's jaws.

"Edith! That's not nice." He gave a placating and sorrowful glance to Sam. "I'm sorry. I don't know what gets into her. I'll put her in the bathroom again when I get back." He started out the door. "I left an ashtray on the coffee table, just for you."

"*Grazie.*" Sam lit up and settled into the couch. Thad glanced back at him and suddenly didn't feel as weighed down by food as he had. Now he was experiencing a new kind of hunger, one he hoped would be completely satiated in about an hour or so.

After Thad made Edith comfortable in the bathroom with the usual trappings—her little shearling bed and her Kong toy stuffed with peanut butter—he stopped to admire Sam on the couch, his head lolled back and his eyes closed. He had finished his cigarette, and a haze of blue smoke hung in the air. Normally Thad would have described the cloud as "gross," but Sam smoking, oddly, was a turn-on for him. He longed to taste the cigarette on Sam's tongue.

Quietly Thad slipped out of his jeans, T-shirt, and sweater and walked slowly over to Sam completely naked, hoping he wouldn't open his eyes as he approached. He also hoped Sam had not fallen asleep.

Sam didn't open his eyes as he neared, nor did he open them when Thad straddled his lap and sank down on him, their chests and stomachs crushed together. The feeling of being naked atop Sam's fully-clothed body was electric, and Thad got an immediate hard-on. He knew Sam wasn't asleep when his lips curled in a slight grin and he reached back and began very gently running his hands up and down Thad's back and ass, pausing to rub at the bumps in his spine and flicker over his crack. Thad thought the light touch and Sam's nearness was about enough to make him come, but he would not let that happen, not for a long while, anyway. Thad leaned forward to flick his tongue in and out of Sam's ear and to nibble at his earlobe. He buried his face in Sam's neck, burrowing in, inhaling the scent of him: sweet sweat, smoke, and garlic. Under other circumstances Thad might have thought of these aromas as odors, but tonight they were magic, an olfactory pipeline leading straight to Thad's genitals. For Thad they made a direct connection to both Sam's heart and his libido. The roughness of Sam's beard grating against his skin just about put Thad over the top. He pulled back—reluctantly—and moved his lips to Sam's mouth. They ground their lips together, their tongues dueling, tasting each other and ratcheting up the passion. All the while both Sam and Thad frantically unbuttoned Sam's shirt and pulled it off—the mat of fur there felt like heaven against Thad's smooth pecs. Then they shifted and bucked to get down Sam's pants.

Sam's erection was poised now at Thad's crack, and for several minutes Thad waged an internal war between lust and common sense, both putting up the good fight. One part of him, the little devil on his shoulder, was telling him *Just sink down on it, feel that dick inside me, skin against skin*. This was a luxury no amount of common sense could convince Thad he really didn't want. It would be crazy beautiful to just go with the moment and lower himself slowly on Sam's cock. What were the odds, anyway? Thad had always been careful, and so he most likely would not be exposing Sam to anything.

And Sam? *Come on, much as I like this guy and maybe am falling for him, and as much as he turns me on, I really don't know anything about him. He could have been the town whore back in Sicily or could have gone to bathhouses and sex parties every night when he moved to New York.*

The thought of Sam doing such things caused a fiery flame of jealousy to ignite in Thad, enough to cause a pang of nausea to swell in his gut and the temperature of his passion to cool by several degrees.

He pulled back and grinned at Sam, all but salivating at the thought of Sam inside him, and said, "Oh man, I want you in me so bad, but you have to give me a minute here."

Sam eyed him and nodded. "Of course." He added hoarsely, "Hurry."

Thad rushed to the bedside table, only a few feet away, and snatched a bottle of lube and some Magnum condoms he had bought just for Sam, then rushed right back to him. He knelt between Sam's spread and hairy thighs and took his cock in his mouth, lubing it up with spit and working his hand in motion with his bobbing head. Sam wriggled his fingers through Thad's red hair, pulling just hard enough to make it hurt, but it was pain Thad welcomed. It felt as though Sam's dick swelled by at least another inch or two with Thad's ministrations, in both length and girth. The musky smell of Sam's balls was causing precum to leak from Thad's own dick and pool on the hardwood below. Part of him wanted to pause to lick it up. He was losing himself in the act, not even sure who was moaning anymore. Was he really grunting as he gobbled Sam's cock, pausing every so often to take each ball in his mouth gently, like an egg?

Sam cried out. "Oh, you keep that up and it'll be over...at least just for now. That what you want?"

Sam's dick throbbed in his mouth, and he knew the end was upon them. They were *almost* at the point of no return. He wanted so much to bring Sam off this way, to watch his cum spurting out. He wanted to rub his cum all over his face and bury his head next to Sam's ebbing cock.

But a tiny part of his mind told him it would be even better if he did what he had started out to do. So, with a great force of will, he pushed himself away, like a starving man away from his favorite food, brought the condom wrapper to his mouth, ripped it open, and slowly rolled the latex over Sam's cock.

He stood, straddled Sam, and smiling all the while, slid down the length of Sam's manhood, feeling it fill him, stretching. He wanted it so bad, there was no pain, only the most delirious pleasure as Sam lifted his hips to sink even more deeply inside him.

Thad laughed when he looked down at their stomachs, next to each other. Sam's was covered with Thad's semen. Thad didn't even know when he had come. The pleasure at Sam entering him must have been so great that he simply shot. Sliding down him was one intense, crazy orgasm.

Sam laughed too.

"I didn't even realize it. You feel so good," Thad said, breathless.

Sam smiled and gave a few quick thrusts upward. "You know, that doesn't mean you are off the hook." He thrust several times more, alternating his pace. And even though he had already come, it still felt delicious to Thad, and already his dick was slowly jerking back up to attention.

Sam stopped. "Let's finish this on the bed." Without waiting for a reply, he grasped Thad's ass and hoisted them both up and off the couch, where he waddled over to the bed, holding Thad firmly on himself, and lowered him gently, if a bit awkwardly, onto the comforter. He got Thad's legs up on his shoulders, splaying his thighs up close to Thad's crack, kissed him deeply, then rose up to begin pounding into him ruthlessly.

When he came, Sam raised his head and howled.

Chapter Seven

OCTOBER

Thad wanted to surprise Sam. As he walked Edith near Green Lake, he glanced over at the warm lights coming out of the Blue Moon Café and thought that he really hadn't stopped in alone as he had the night they met. Wouldn't it be romantic to repeat that evening, complete with capping it off in Thad's apartment? The thought heated him, both in his heart and, well, lower. He could wear the same clothes he had worn that night and maybe even encourage a bit of role-playing, so that they were new to each other once more.

Yes, we are a couple now. We really are. Ever since the night Thad had met the rest of the Lupino family a month ago, the two men had been practically inseparable. Work was the only thing that kept them apart. They spent nearly every night together, except for a few times when Sam had had to make a couple of out-of-town trips to visit his grandmother—he called her his *nana*—in New York. Sam had explained that Nana was happy in Queens, where she had a small apartment in an assisted living home, and was physically unable to make the trip to the Pacific Northwest with the remainder of the clan. She had raised a fuss when the family wanted to move and had only agreed to it when Sam and the others promised her they would visit regularly.

The only other nights they had not slept next to each other was when Sam was simply too tired from his work to come over. Even though Thad had told him that it didn't matter if they had sex or not—having him near was enough—Sam explained that sometimes he slept better and more restfully if he was by himself. The explanation made sense to Thad, but it was still something he hoped to change.

Thad hoped that, on one of the trips east, Sam would take him along.

But tonight, as far as he knew, Sam was in town and working. Edith pranced along the lakefront trail a little ahead of him, stopping every once in a while to sniff at something particularly crucial on the ground or a tree trunk. The dog seemed to enjoy her chilly nighttime walks and behaved fearlessly, even though patches of the trail itself were quite dark at night. Thad provided her with a variety of sweaters to warm her on their outings. Sadly, Edith remained the one sore spot in his relationship with Sam. The dog's dislike for the man had not decreased any since Thad had first brought him home. Familiarity did not lessen the snapping, growling, and barking Edith seemed unable to control whenever Sam arrived. The boyfriend and the dog had, however, reached an uneasy truce. Thad no longer put her in the bathroom when Sam came over, but she took her leave of them immediately when he did, as if in a snit, and would stay on her tiny bathroom bed until she was sure Sam was gone. Sam had said, with a wry smile, that Edith was alpha, and she was just ensuring her place in the pecking order. He really didn't seem to mind.

But tonight, at least for a while, Edith had her master all to herself. If Thad hadn't been so hopelessly in love with both Sam and Edith, he might have considered getting rid of Edith, but the thought, even momentary, broke his heart.

He appreciated this quiet time along the lakefront with her. The October air was cold, yet brisk and invigorating. Steam rose off the lake's dark waters. Wind rustled the few dry remaining leaves that clung the most stubbornly to the trees surrounding the water.

And the water itself looked magnificent tonight, shimmering in the light of a huge harvest moon, full and glowing like a jack-o'-lantern.

*

He prowls Capitol Hill once more. It's still early evening, and the revelers have not yet made their appearance. He bides his time in a residential alley, grooming himself and curling into a small ball near an apartment building dumpster. If anyone should happen upon him, they would think he was only a stray. Curling into a tight ball like this is deceptive, concealing both his size and ferocity. His eyes—black as glistening coal—stare up at the large full moon, now partially obscured by thin streams of cloud. He longs to bay at that moon, but always the hunter in him comes first, and he realizes even the slightest disturbance to his prey could mean he might go hungry tonight.

He has plans for later, when the revelers have trickled down to a determined and desperate few. On one of these, he will prey. One of these, he thinks, will no longer have to live a life ruled by his own twisted desires. One of these will no longer be around to spread disease and corruption.

He licks his chops in anticipation and closes his eyes to wait for the moon to shrink and the darkness to become inkier.

*

Thad stood in front of the mirror, wearing the same outfit he had worn that first night he made his way into the then-brand-new restaurant known as the Blue Moon Café. His black jeans, combat boots, and vintage Brit-rocker T-shirt made him look slim, mean, and sexy, he thought. *With no amount of vanity...* Thad laughed and turned away from the mirror. *Call me a hopeless romantic if you will, but I think Sam will love this idea. I'll even ask him to recreate what he cooked for me that first night.* Thad recalled how Sam had custom-made his dinner. Thad thought, sadly, that the culinary recreation might not be possible. Since its opening the restaurant had become hugely popular, in the neighborhood and well beyond. The write-up in *Seattle Metropolitan* magazine and positive reviews on sites like Yelp.com brought even more crowds in, making weekend reservations a must and weeknight ones a good idea.

But Sam will find me a small table, no matter how busy they are. I am, how you say, a VIP.

Thad took Edith out for one more quick bathroom break, grabbed his leather jacket—the one thing he did *not* need that first night—and set out for the Blue Moon Café.

Just as he was fishing his key out of his jeans pocket to lock his door, he heard the chirp of his landline phone. He debated whether he should go back to answer it and in the end decided to return just to check the Caller ID. It might be Sam.

Edith hopped hopefully from the couch when Thad reentered the apartment. He knew in her mind all that mattered was that he had returned, not the length of time he was gone. She began jumping up and down on his legs, excited to welcome him back home.

"Sorry, sweetheart, but I'll only be here a minute."

He glanced down at the cordless phone's display and saw that Jared was calling. The two had become, as Thad had hoped, friends over the past month. Jared had even trained Thad so he could work on the front desk at Lifelong AIDS Alliance, getting him out of the warehouse, where filling bags with food quickly had become undeniably monotonous, no matter how charitable. When he wasn't with Sam, he was usually with Jared, and the two of them made the rounds of Capitol Hill hotspots, Thad just looking for a good dirty martini and Jared looking for a dirty good time. The latter was the reason the pair usually ended up separated before the night was over. Still, Jared had a great sense of humor, and Thad did like his company, in spite of the fact that he never quite completely got the message that Thad was not interested in doing anything sexual with him. But that was okay too, since there were plenty who were interested...and the word "no" did not seem to be in Jared's vocabulary.

Thad snatched up the phone before it went to the answering machine. "What's up, slut?"

Jared snickered. "Oh, shut up! You're just jealous because you have the same old corned beef hash every night and I'm dining at a smorgasbord."

"You're incorrigible. Did you call for a reason?"

"Well! Excuse me for being friendly! Yes, I was, actually. There's a full moon tonight, and I'm in the mood to howl. The Eagle is having a full-moon party tonight, and I think there will be a lot of guys out in assless chaps. Want in on it?"

Thad sighed. He said no to Jared a lot, simply because he was usually with Sam. He hated to do it again. But the sight of leather men in chaps with their asses bare no longer thrilled him as it once had. He had enough hot visuals in his own home to keep him more than satisfied.

"You don't have to do anything, buddy. Just enjoy the eye candy. You're not too married for that, are you?"

"Well, I'm not dead. But I was actually on my way out the door to go see Sam. I thought I'd surprise him and walk in as an ordinary restaurant patron tonight."

"There is nothing ordinary about you, sweetheart."

"That means a lot, coming from you. Thanks. But I do have to send my regrets. Sorry."

"It's okay. I'm sure I'll find someone to keep me company."

"Of that I have no doubt. Have fun and give me a call in the morning. Not too early."

"You mean, like, when I'm getting home?" Jared laughed.

"Exactly. Have a good time."

"You too. And if you change your mind, just text me. You can join up with me at almost any point. Well, *almost* any point." Jared paused as if thinking. "I take that back. You *can* join me at any point. The more, the merrier!"

They both were laughing as they said their goodbyes.

As Thad walked to the Blue Moon Café, he forgot all about Jared. Sam was waiting for him, whether he knew it or not, and that crowded everything else from his thoughts.

As he entered the restaurant, Thad immediately sensed something was different. Sure, there was the same lively Saturday-night crowd the restaurant had been enjoying as it was making itself known in Seattle. There were the sounds of glasses clinking, flatware on china, people talking and laughing. The same smells hung in the air—delicious—garlic, basil, and onion predominating. But it took Thad only a second to process what was wrong.

He looked around again at the bartender and the waitstaff and tried in vain to find a familiar face. Thad knew that, of course, the family had hired additional help to accommodate their growing success, but it was rare that he stopped by when at least one of the Lupinos was not working.

Tonight none of them were.

His heart fell as he hoped against hope that at least Sam was in the kitchen, whipping up some fresh gnocchi or something.

A young woman with short spiky blonde hair smiled and approached the reception desk. "Hi! Welcome to the Blue Moon! Do you have a reservation?"

How could she not know who he was? He was the owner's boyfriend, for cryin' out loud. But he would be even more upset if Sam wasn't here.

"No, I don't."

She dialed her beaming smile down just a notch. "Oh. Sorry. We are completely booked tonight." She glanced behind her at the bar. "We might be able to squeeze you in at the bar, and if you want something to eat there, we'll be happy to set you up." She peered closer. "But even that, right now, is packed." She turned back to him. "Do you wanna stay?"

"Actually, I just dropped by to see Sam. Is he in the kitchen? You can just tell him Thad is here."

The young woman nodded, and then her expression went blank. "Sam's not in tonight."

"Oh?"

"Yeah, the whole family took the night off. They do that sometimes."

"Do you know if they're back in the apartment?"

A couple had come in behind Thad, and he could feel their impatience at his back like a hot breath.

"I wouldn't know. Maybe when I have a minute, I could go check for you or see if anyone else knows. You a friend of Sam's?"

"I'm his boyfriend." Thad couldn't contain the pride in his voice as he identified his relationship.

"Well, if you want to hang on for a bit, I'll see what I can do to help out. But I have to tell you, we are swamped tonight." Thad felt dismissed as she leaned over to peer behind him. "Hi! Welcome to the Blue Moon! Do you have a reservation tonight?"

Thad wandered away. A line had already formed behind him.

He stepped out into the cool night air, disappointed and, at the same time, a little hurt. Why hadn't Sam mentioned anything to him about not being around? A similar thing had happened once or twice before, but it was during the week, so Thad hadn't been too concerned. But they usually spent weekends together. Sam knew that.

Before I go getting all hurt, maybe I should find out what's up. Maybe he is indeed in the apartment with the rest of the family. Maybe they just needed a break. Nothing to get upset about, at least not until I know.

Thad pulled out his cell and punched in the number for the apartment. The phone on the other end simply rang and rang, at least fifteen times, before Thad disconnected. *Odd. There's usually voice mail.*

He tried Sam's cell, and the call went immediately into voice mail, as if the phone had been shut off.

Thad wrapped his arms around himself as a chill wind blew at him from across the lake. He looked up at the full moon above the water, smaller now and in a different place from when he had walked earlier with Edith, and felt confused, a little angry, and hurt.

Where was Sam?

*

The streets have quieted. Traffic has slowed to a few cars now and then instead of the steady stream of honking and revving vehicles, circling endlessly to find parking. Voices on the streets have decreased to an echo, borne away quickly by the night breeze. The streets are almost deserted, the wind sending the trash skittering along the sidewalk to pile up in gutters and along curbs. A light drizzle falls and makes his coat sleek as he prowls the streets more heedlessly. His black sheen is one with the night, which is now full dark. Clouds have obscured the moon.

Still, he travels mostly alleys or stays close to buildings, hidden by their shadows.

One or two prospects pass by him, and he eyes them hungrily, then rejects them. He can smell the stink of addiction on them—or disease—and knows the meat will be tainted. The rain cuts away the car exhaust and fumes, damping them, so his senses are more attuned to his prey.

His ears perk up as he smells them first, then hears their footsteps coming up Pine Street. They smell young, healthy, and he knows one of them will make for a very satisfying feast. He stands up from his crouch, shakes his fur, and thinks maybe he should not limit himself to only one. After all, he feeds like this but once a month.

He slips back into the entrance to a vintage clothing storefront and listens. The men have just emerged from a nearby bathhouse, a place called Club Z.

"Hey! Would you wait up?"

One man runs after the other, and the second one, the blond, is amused. Oh, to have the simplicity of being chased by a mere human being! Lover boy, you have no idea...

"What? What do you want?"

The man running closes the distance, and the creature listens to his rough breathing, knowing he has run for a while.

"I just thought it would be fun to spend a little more time together."

"Didn't we just do that? Back at the bathhouse?"

"I know," the one man whines. "And that was fun. Really fun." His laugh is low, tainted with filth. "But I just thought maybe we could cuddle a little, you know? I live over on Denny, or we could go to your place, if you're close. I just want to fall asleep next to you."

There are a few minutes of silence. Then he hears: "I need to get up early, and I sleep better by myself. Look, I'll give you a call."

Footsteps retreat. He peers around a corner and watches as one man continues east up Pine Street and the other stands immobile, watching him go. Finally the tall blond man vanishes into the night.

The other, a tight little dark-haired guy with a moustache and dark skin, stays frozen to his spot, as if in shock, watching until long after his "friend" is no longer visible. Then he leans against a restaurant's plate glass window and begins to weep softly.

On silent paws, the creature creeps around a corner and disappears into an alley. There he knocks over a stack of cans to make some clatter. As he suspects, the noise draws the guy with the moustache, and he peers around the corner. The monster clearly sees the man, but the man does not see the monster. He ventures a few steps into the alley, as if curious about what made the noise.

And the monster is upon him, fangs bared, going first for the throat so the man cannot emit even a little scream.

*

Jared felt bad. He had had an amazing time with Hector in his room at Club Z, and the pair had fucked in every conceivable position, their bodies becoming slicked with sweat, their heart rates accelerating, and their passion peaking together, but only after about a solid hour of rough sex. Even though Jared's dance card was always full, this was one encounter that was outstanding enough to remember for a long time.

But after, when they had slumped against each other on the cum- and sweat-drenched sheets, Hector began talking about how "special" Jared was and how he so much wanted to see him again. "You are my idea of the perfect boyfriend. I am going to call into work tomorrow so I can spend the rest of the night with you. And then in the morning, we can get up, and I will treat you to breakfast."

He had scared Jared. Hector's desperation and clinginess radiated off the handsome man like the scent of his perspiration. Jared had come to Club Z for the simple reason that he wanted no-entanglement sex. Casual sex. A hookup. A hot, anonymous fuck. He didn't need—or want—a boyfriend, husband, lover, partner.

Well, he did. But the object of his desire was taken, and Jared knew he might never become available. Quickly he put images of red hair and porcelain skin out of his head.

But as he headed home along the lonely streets of Capitol Hill at going on 3:00 a.m., he couldn't help but feel sad and sorry for Hector. The guy had run after him, for Christ's sake, and when he had left him behind on the street corner, he could see the tears glistening in his eyes.

I'm such a softie. I should just go home. I'll only encourage him if I go back. But the sad brown eyes, dewy with tears, nagged at Jared. He had never been able to turn away a stray and was always first to play Good Samaritan if the opportunity arose. He shook his head, laughing ruefully at his own inability to be tough. He turned around and started to head back. *I'll regret this. He'll never stop calling me. And when I do make it clear I'm not interested, he'll get mad, just like so many others. Am I sure I want to do this?*

Jared slowed his footsteps, considering. But the pull of Hector's pleading face and the image of him standing alone on the street in the rain left Jared no choice. He picked up his pace.

He was a little relieved to find Hector no longer standing on the corner where he had left him. Perhaps the guy was stronger than Jared had thought. Maybe he had gone home, or back to Club Z, to start looking all over again. Jared could relate to that, having done the same himself on more than a few occasions.

A sound issued forth from the alley...like a snarl, followed by a whine. Was a dog back there? Was it hurt?

Jared! Jared! Go home right now! I don't need another rescue animal! Two dogs in a one-bedroom! I have enough!

But just like the pull of Hector's tear-soaked eyes, Jared couldn't resist the thought of an animal in trouble.

He hurried to the alley's mouth.

Jared gasped. Some kind of beast, its eyes glistening black and feral, looked up at him, the fiery gaze pulling Jared right into what he felt were the depths of hell. A scream lodged in his throat, terror and breathlessness holding it there, a silent hostage.

Jared began to tremble as he heard the low growl of the creature taking form in the darkness, almost like an apparition. The growl was a warning, and Jared finally could see why. An arm, a human arm, hung out of the beast's mouth. Blood and bits of flesh dripped from the limb. The rest of the body, shredded, black blood pooling on alley bricks beneath, lay at the monster's feet.

It all seemed unreal. Dizzy, Jared grabbed on to some bricks for support.

What was this thing? It looked like a wolf but was too big for a wolf, and its pose suggested a crouch, almost like a human form.

Jared's mind went blank from shock and horror. He watched, frozen, as the creature dropped the half-eaten arm from its mouth, stared slack-jawed as it hunkered down on its haunches, poised to spring.

Finally, as his awe- and dumbstruck brain hurriedly smashed the pieces of the puzzle together, Jared screamed and turned to run.

The creature's breath was hot on his heels.

Chapter Eight

Thad experienced a miserable night of sleep. Tossing and turning, mind racing, the few moments here and there he drifted off had been destroyed by nightmares, the dreams so terrifying he awakened several times drenched in sweat, gasping, or even emitting a muffled scream. Only images remained from the dreams, but they were powerful enough to chill Thad. Pictures of moons, claws, fangs, and blood tortured him until finally, at about 6:00 a.m., he forced himself to get up from his sweat-soaked sheets. Trying to sleep was pointless.

Edith snored softly atop the pillow next to his head, curled into a tight ball. *At least someone isn't plagued by nightmares...and doubt...and disappointment.*

As Thad ground coffee beans and poured the grounds and a carafe of water into the coffeemaker, he had no doubt from where his restlessness and vivid bad dreams had come: Sam. Where had he been last night? Why hadn't he told Thad he would be taking the night off? And where was the rest of the family? If they were all going to be away, wouldn't that be a remarkable enough fact that Sam would find it worthy of mentioning to his boyfriend?

Unless...

Unless Sam was hiding something.

Oh, please don't get started with the paranoia again! I always do this. Have a little confidence in Sam and our relationship. Have a little confidence—for once—in myself.

Thad poured himself a mug of coffee and sat at his little breakfast bar, heaping three teaspoons of sugar into the steaming black liquid, along with a dollop of half-and-half.

Sam will probably supply the answers I need in short order. Once he gets back. From wherever it is he went...from wherever he couldn't be bothered to let me know he was going...

Thad shook his head and stirred. Sure, there might have been a logical reason for Sam and his whole family to disappear on a busy-for-the-restaurant Saturday night, but what could it be? An emergency? The grandmother in Queens had fallen ill? A sudden urge to visit the Olympic Peninsula, to see the mountains and ocean by the light of the full moon? Thad laughed out loud, but there was no mirth in it. He felt alone and excluded.

Insecurity and doubt ate at him, and he had to wonder, really, if Sam wasn't hiding something from him. Why else would he disappear without a word?

But what? Another lover? A wife? Was Graziela really *not* his sister? Were they, in fact, Domenic's mother and father? Did they have some sort of arrangement Sam didn't yet have the courage to share with him?

That's crazy. Why, after two months, wouldn't he tell me? And why would that cause the whole family to disappear? But what else could he be hiding? Something darker?

One of Thad's nightmare images—fangs coated in blood—rose up to chill and torment him. He had no idea what this image had to do with his fears and suspicion regarding Sam.

The coffee, even in spite of the sugar and cream, tasted hot, sour, and acidic as it went down. It served only to make him more jittery.

He needed to talk to someone. The sky outside was only a dull gray, the sun just beginning its journey up and over the Cascade Mountains. He glanced at the clock and saw it wasn't even six thirty yet. Who could he call at this hour? Who could he phone who wouldn't bite his head off for waking him at such an ungodly hour on a Sunday morning?

Thad smiled. *Jared*. If he knew Jared as he thought he did, Jared would just be getting in. Jared may have crawled into his own bed after a night of debauchery, but Thad was willing to bet his friend had not yet drifted off to sleep.

He grabbed his cell and pulled it toward him, held down the three button to be connected with Jared.

But all he got was his voice mail. Jared never liked to stay long at any one-night stand's place and never permitted them to hang around for breakfast when he brought them home to his own apartment, but this Sunday must have had an unusual outcome because Jared was not answering.

A pang of totally unexpected jealousy shot through Thad. *Great! Now I can wonder where someone else is!*

He shook his head, grabbed his coffee, and went over to the small area defined as a living room by the love seat and TV on a stand. He picked up the remote and pointed it at the TV, hoping to obliterate his fears with the morning news.

And there, right before his eyes, was horror so extreme, it immediately jolted him from his cocoon of lethargy and despair. His heart thundered in his chest as the anchor's calm voice recounted the grisly details of yet another killing. Once again a man had been brutally murdered in Seattle's gay neighborhood, Capitol Hill. *Where Jared lives! Where Jared was out prowling around last night!* Thad shivered, straining to hear the anchor's voice over the pounding of blood in his ears. Once again the murder had all the hallmarks of a beastly slaying—replete with partially eaten flesh—yet no one recalled seeing any bears or coyotes roaming around loose in the very urban and very populated neighborhood. As a precaution, police and wildlife authorities were planning on conducting a search of Capitol Hill's Volunteer Park later today.

Perhaps the most chilling detail of the whole report was not only the fact that this was the third killing of what appeared to be gay men, but that "the victim's identity is being withheld pending notification of the family."

The coffee Thad had drunk swirled around in his stomach, morphing into acidic bile and making him nauseous.

After pacing the studio for what seemed like hours, Thad took Edith out for a quick walk around his block and decided he couldn't just sit and wait for Jared to call.

He's probably okay. I mean, what are the odds?

Thad felt himself pale at the thought of those same odds. There was some maniac targeting gay men. Jared was gay. The maniac had killed last night. *In Jared's 'hood...and Jared was out last night.* Thad tried to tell himself there were hundreds, if not thousands, of other gay men out last night, many of them in the same Seattle neighborhood where the killing had taken place. Any one of them could have been the victim.

Not Jared. Please not Jared.

Thad found he was sweating and realized suddenly how much he cared about his new friend. Bad enough to hear news of a fellow human being, and fellow gay man at that, being savaged, but when it was someone you knew, someone who made you laugh, and someone you cared about... Well, it made Thad's stomach churn.

In spite of the early morning chill in the air and the gray sky and mist, Thad felt hot, his heart racing. He couldn't recall a time when he had been this worried about someone.

He dispensed with fretting over bus schedules and the hit-or-miss of getting one to take him down to Capitol Hill early on a Sunday morning. Even though financially it was out of his reach, he took Edith back to his apartment and called a cab. Emotionally, he couldn't afford *not* to make use of what he considered, under other circumstances, an extravagance.

He was too worried to bother with a shower or, really, any personal grooming. While he waited for the cab, he threw on a pair of old Levi's, a flannel shirt, and hiking boots. All the while he tried to imagine a sleepy Jared opening the door to him, wondering what had brought him to his apartment at this early hour on a Sunday. And all the while he tried to keep his terror at bay. He fought with himself not to imagine the door going unanswered. Fought not to picture in his mind a grainy newspaper photo of Jared on the front page of the *Seattle Times* with a headline proclaiming "Latest Victim."

The ride from Green Lake to Capitol Hill seemed to take hours, with Thad wringing his hands the entire way. He tried to swallow and found his mouth was dry. He even resorted to whispering prayers to himself. He silently prodded the cab driver to go faster, the very scenery to blur.

He had to know.

The ride itself took only ten minutes, but Thad was ready to leap from the cab before it even came to a complete stop in front of Jared's redbrick apartment house. He threw some cash on the seat beside his driver, told him to keep the change, and jumped from the vehicle.

The cab driver pulled away quickly, as if he were afraid Thad would change his mind about the big tip.

Thad looked up, praying he would see something at one of Jared's apartment windows. But the darkened windowpanes mocked him. He saw no movement, no signs of light.

No signs of life, I mean. Oh, don't be so melodramatic! Just get up to the front door and ring Jared's buzzer.

Thad followed his own advice, leaning on the buzzer beneath the little label that read J. Holmes again and again, for what seemed like ten minutes. The silence he got back in return taunted him, ratcheting up his worry. Suddenly he was certain Jared, with his promiscuous, careless ways, was the latest victim of this maniac savagely targeting gay men in Seattle.

Thad hung his head in defeat. There was little more he could do, save for sit here on the front stoop and hope to look up and see Jared coming down the street, whistling a happy tune, hands in pockets, filled with recent carnal memories and oblivious to the horror of last night.

Just then he got a break. A young woman, loaded down with a laundry basket, pushed open the front door. Thad moved aside to let her pass, then snatched the plate glass door before it closed and locked.

Taking the stairs two and three at a time, he rushed up the three stories to Jared's front door. He pounded on the wooden surface, knowing it was hopeless, yet hoping Jared had simply not heard the buzzer or was busy with a trick and was ignoring it. He didn't care if he interrupted slumber or sex. He just wanted to know Jared was alive.

When Jared opened the door just a crack and peered out at him, relief coursed through Thad, so intense it was like he had been injected with a drug. Jared's blue eyes were wild, and his skin looked pale and clammy. He wore only a pair of faded boxer shorts and a Seattle Sonics T-shirt.

What was wrong? He looked at Thad like he didn't know him for a few seconds. Then when he realized who it was, a glimmer of a smile passed over his features. Shaky, but the smile was there. He opened the door a little wider and then stuck his head out into the hallway to give a quick surveillance in both directions. Grabbing Thad roughly by his forearm, Jared pulled him into the apartment and slammed the door behind him.

Jared was trembling, and Thad couldn't get over how pale he looked. Thad wondered if his friend had gotten into drugs. Crystal meth was a pretty common scourge of the gay community in Seattle, and with the kind of lifestyle Jared led, it wouldn't have surprised Thad if the guy had added speed to his sexual repertoire. Still, Jared was such a gentle soul; it just didn't seem like him. And from how Jared had regaled him with his almost constant stream of sexual escapades, his friend didn't seem to need any mood enhancers. Still, what else could be causing the obvious paranoia, the shaking, and the clammy, pale skin?

Terror?

"Did you see anything weird outside?"

Thad shook his head and took a few more steps into Jared's one-bedroom apartment. One of his dogs, a pit bull mix, came out to greet him, panting and jumping up on him. Absently, Thad patted the dog's head and struggled to maintain his balance.

"Get down, Jack!" Jared's voice was sharper than Thad had ever heard it, and the dog scurried away. Thad could hear it join the other dog—a rat terrier—in the bedroom.

"Well, did you?"

"No, I didn't see anything except one of your neighbors carrying a bushel of laundry. That's not weird, is it?"

"Come in. Come in." Jared led Thad over to a couch he had positioned beneath a picture window that looked out on a large pine tree in the backyard. The sky was light and pearl gray. The outdoor scene, almost serene, seemed at odds with the anxious mood inside. Jared flopped down on the quilt-covered couch, pulled a pack of Marlboro Lights from the coffee table, and with shaking fingers, lit one up.

"You smoke?" Thad was stunned.

"Used to. I quit. Four years ago. But I need this now. It calms me. I hope it doesn't bother you." First Sam and now Jared. Thad wondered if he shouldn't take up the bad habit himself, just to be one of the boys.

"Jared...what's wrong?"

Jared sat and smoked, stared off into the distance. After a bit he said, "You wouldn't believe me if I told you." One of the dogs wandered in from the bedroom, the rat terrier this time. He hopped up on the couch and snuggled up to Jared's thigh. The smoke didn't seem to bother him.

"Hey, Fred." Jared stroked the dog.

"Jared, what's going on?"

Jared took a few more drags on the cigarette, then ground it out in an ashtray Thad had yet to notice. It was nearly overflowing with butts. Jared sighed and shook his head. "Last night..."

Jared stopped talking. His eyes sparkled with fear. He seemed unable to find the breath to put behind any more words.

Jesus! What's going on? Did Jared get into some kind of bad sex scene last night? Had he been beaten or forced to do something against his will?

Thad searched Jared's face and exposed skin for some signs of injury but found nothing. "What happened last night? You can tell me. I'm your friend." Thad laid what he hoped was a comforting hand on Jared's thigh.

Jared picked up the cigarette pack, considered it, then threw it back down to the coffee table's glass surface. "Last night I saw something horrible."

Jared didn't say anything for a long time. He simply sat and stared into the distance, as if he was seeing something only he could see. Whatever internal movie was running before Jared's eyes, it was obviously deeply troubling. Jared had always been the happy-go-lucky one of the two of them, the one with the jokes, the dirty mind, the attitude that he could take whatever came his way. But now he looked like a terrified man, as if something had so traumatized him it morphed his entire demeanor, making of Jared a sad, shriveled thing, too frightened to do much more than stare and occasionally tremble.

"Tell me," Thad whispered.

Jared slid up next to Thad, positioning himself so he could put his head on Thad's chest. "Last night I saw something you won't believe."

"What?" Thad could not imagine what Jared had seen. Did this have something to do with the killings lately? Had Jared been a witness? No, that was too far-fetched. Things like that didn't happen to people one knew, right?

Jared sucked in a great, quivering breath. "I was out last night, you know? Playing the tomcat as usual. Met up with several guys at Club Z, had some fun, and then I hooked up with this really hot little Latino. Man, he was tireless!" A flicker of a grin worked its way across Jared's features, then vanished. "I left him on the street. He wanted to come home with me. Oh God, how I wish he had!" Jared grew quiet again.

"But you know me, patron saint of lost causes. I couldn't just leave the guy standing there in the street. He was on the verge of tears, for Christ's sake. So I went back. And that's when I saw Hector again..." Jared's voice trailed off, and it almost seemed the temperature in the room dropped by a few degrees.

It was quiet once more for a while. But Thad didn't want to push his friend.

Finally, when Jared spoke again, his voice was dead.

"You heard, probably, that there was another killing last night. It was Hector, the guy I hooked up with...and left there to die. When I came back, I didn't see him and thought he'd gone home or back to the bathhouse. I was about to go home when I heard a sound come from the alley...like a growl and a whimper. I went to look." Jared lifted his head to stare into Thad's eyes. Jared's own eyes were alive with fear.

"The thing had Hector. It had ripped him apart. There was blood everywhere."

Jared began to weep, and Thad, stunned, could do little more than pat his friend's back.

"What thing?"

Jared sat up and, with shaking hands, lit another cigarette. He stared into the cloud of blue-gray smoke. Jared closed his eyes. "You wouldn't believe me if I told you."

Thad didn't know what to think. Had his friend lost his mind? What was in there, anyway? What was he seeing as that endless loop of horror memories playing in his head? "I trust you, man. Just tell me."

"I saw a werewolf."

Chapter Nine

Monday morning Sam went outside the café to pick up a newspaper from the box on the corner. It had been a rough weekend, and he'd gotten little sleep. His eyes burned, and his muscles felt like those of an old man, stretched beyond endurance, aching. He shuffled like so many of the old guys back in Sicily as he approached the mailbox, then laughed and forced himself to pick up his pace, even though it hurt to do so.

He slid some quarters into the box and opened the creaking front to take out a paper, then gasped when he saw the headline on the front page—

Is a Werewolf Stalking Seattle?

Sam's legs grew so weak and rubbery that he had to sit down suddenly on the curb. His heart thudded in his chest. He stared at the headline until his eyes blurred, disbelieving.

When he could compose himself, just barely, he scanned the story, reading over the details of how an unidentified witness had come forward to tell a tale of having seen what appeared to be an "enormous wolflike" creature in an alley in Capitol Hill, still feasting on the remains of his latest victim, Hector Garcia.

Bile splashed at the back of his throat. Sam forced himself to stand on unsteady legs and, as best he could, hurried back inside, whispering, "The family needs to know."

*

Thad needed comfort. He had spent all of Sunday dispensing that precious commodity to Jared and felt he had none left to expend on himself. The day before had been such a drain that today, Monday, exhaustion ate at Thad. He was in one of those states where he was simply too tired to sleep. The concept of being too tired to sleep was one he had never made much sense of, but now, even when he tried to nap—his body achy with weariness—his mind kept racing every time he lay down, as if he were sabotaging himself.

He had spent all yesterday morning and afternoon with Jared, returning to his Green Lake studio only to pick up Edith, who couldn't be left by herself for hours on end. She had more self-control than Thad in many ways, but her bladder was too small to be ignored for long periods. Thad had hurried back to his place on Jared's Vespa to pick up Edith, put her in a backpack—thank heaven for toy dogs!—and come back to Jared, who was desperately afraid of being alone.

The pair had spent almost the entire day on the couch, sitting close. Thad alternately comforted Jared with soothing words and reassurances that he was safe and tried to distract him with old movies and junk food. Nothing seemed to help much. His friend's sense of humor had been replaced by fear and paranoia.

Finally Thad had convinced him to go to the closest police precinct and report what he had seen. Jared had been more than reluctant. "They'll think I'm nuts!" he had protested.

"You *are* nuts, sweetheart. But that doesn't change what you saw. Now, let's go. I am not taking no for an answer on this one." It was the only time Thad had been firm with Jared, but he knew if he didn't take charge, he would never persuade Jared to leave the apartment. The police were initially interested, but their interest faded when Jared began talking about having seen a werewolf. Interest had turned to humoring, and Thad felt embarrassed for Jared. The detective they spoke to dutifully logged in Jared's recollections, gave him his card, and advised him to stay close in case the department had further questions.

As they left the station, a reporter from one of the Seattle papers caught up with them, and in spite of Thad's advice not to talk to her, Jared spilled out his whole story to the reporter. Thad thought it was a mistake, knowing the field day the press would have with Jared's hair-raising and sensational story, but he was unable to dam the flow of words springing forth from his friend's mouth once he had a receptive audience.

Thad had spent the night in Jared's bed. For once no sexual charge passed between them. The night's passage was all about comfort and Thad seeing his friend safely through to the morning's light. All through the night, as the room subtly lightened into dawn, Thad held Jared in his arms. He was Jared's protector not only against werewolves but against nightmares and actual memories that were far worse than any nightmare.

So Thad had not slept. Not a wink. And now he sat on his couch and wondered what he should do. Jared had obviously been so traumatized by what had happened that his mind had played tricks on him. A werewolf? That was laughable. Although the thought did chill him as he recalled the brilliant full moon hanging over Green Lake on Saturday night. But Jared had seen his friend savagely murdered—maybe not the act itself, but the carnage that remained. That enough might be enough to send someone's fragile mind into overdrive, hallucinating some explanation drawn from a horror movie.

Maybe.

But what if Jared had actually seen something monstrous? An animal, perhaps, some freak of nature? Or perhaps the killer was some kind of feral man, filthy and covered in hair. Or maybe Jared had seen nothing at all. The image of his friend torn apart, blood splashing the alley bricks, might be enough to have sent Jared over the edge. A shadow became a wolf man. The bark of a mutt the forlorn howl of a werewolf. It was pretty easy to understand.

Edith slept curled in an armchair perpendicular to the couch. Outside, the afternoon had turned bright, a brilliant Indian-summer day with blue skies highlighting the reds, browns, and yellows of autumn leaves. It all seemed incongruous with the fatigue and turmoil going on not only inside Thad but also with, seemingly, the whole city of Seattle.

One thing was for sure: three gay men had been brutally killed in as many months, and it was hard to ignore that these killings had to somehow be linked.

Running was always a panacea for Thad's body as well as his mind. And even though part of him ached for the oblivion of sleep, he decided maybe by running, he could quell the thoughts racing through his mind and wear out his body so completely, it would have no choice but to surrender to sleep, even if was the middle of the afternoon.

He slid into a pair of shorts, a T-shirt, and his Asics, did a few stretches in the apartment, and headed out for the three-mile trail that circled the lake.

As he was walking back, winded, he passed the Blue Moon Café and stopped. Sam was inside, wiping down the bar, even though the place was not open. The sight of him made Thad's heart pound with even more force. *Where have you been, my man?* Thad stood, watching Sam as he washed wineglasses, dried them, and placed them in a rack above the bar. Someone else he didn't know, a guy about his own age with dirty-blond hair, swept the floor. Graziela stood at the hostess desk, writing, her black hair a curtain obscuring her face.

Before he even knew he had made the decision, Thad's running-sore legs took him to the front door of the café. Sam looked up, and Thad almost turned around, crushed. Sam did not smile when he saw him. He turned and resumed his glass washing with even more intensity and concentration, almost as if he were pretending their eyes had not met.

What's going on?

Thad briefly considered turning around and going home. But his curious nature wouldn't allow that. He took a breath, marched up to the door, and yanked on it.

It was locked.

Graziela looked up, glanced at Thad, then over at Sam. Sam directed his gaze once more toward Thad, and Thad swore he pretended he was seeing Thad for the very first time. His smile was forced and not at all genuine as he hurried to the front door, wiping his hands on his apron.

A pang of nauseous fear settled in Thad's gut. Was it over? Many men had unceremoniously dumped him in the past. Why should Sam be any different? And when they had dumped him, it had usually been like this...with no fanfare, just passive-aggressive ignorance.

Sam unlocked the door and threw it open.

"Thad! What a surprise! Come in, come in."

Sam's voice seemed warm but had an edgy wariness to it Thad could not quite identify and hadn't ever been there before. Sam glanced over his shoulder at Graziela, who disappeared into the back. "You want to come in? We're not open for another few hours, but you are always welcome."

"Thanks." Thad followed Sam into the empty restaurant.

"Bill? Why don't you, um, take five? Go have a smoke?" The guy sweeping the floor smiled in gratitude and hurried outside, already patting his pockets for the accoutrements for his next fix.

"I have a lot to do to get ready for tonight, but I always have time for you." Sam's gaze met Thad's, and Thad relaxed a bit. Sam's words, coupled with the intensity of their eyes meeting, reassured him that Sam was not looking to dump him. At least not yet.

The pair occupied a table that looked out over Green Lake Way and the park beyond it. The water, brilliant deep blue, appeared between trees and swatches of autumn foliage. Now that Thad was sitting across from his boyfriend, he wasn't sure how to ask the questions on his mind without feeling like he was being controlling and overly nosy. But he didn't have a chance to wonder how to begin the conversation because Sam started it for him.

"I must apologize to you." Sam's beefy paws covered Thad's hands. "Things have been very crazy lately. What with having to go out of town this weekend to see my nana and going to the airport this morning, I have hardly had time to take a piss, let alone think about the man I care most about in this whole world."

Sam's description of him made Thad smile, in spite of the torrent of questions forming in the back of his mind. "Is your grandmother okay?"

"Oh yes! She just gets lonely for us, so on Friday we all took a plane out to New York and surprised her for the weekend. You should have seen the tears. But it was a nice time."

"I'm glad." Thad was wary. Again, he wasn't sure how to broach his indignation at being kept out of the loop without sounding like a nag. "Did they tell you I stopped by here on Saturday night? I wanted to surprise you."

"No one mentioned it." Sam looked toward the bar, as if signaling a lot of work still waited for him there. Wasn't he going to explain why he didn't at least let Thad know he'd be gone for the weekend?

"I wish I had known you weren't going to be here. I could have saved myself some trouble." Thad gave Sam a weak smile.

Sam still didn't bite, and Thad could stand waiting around no longer, so he asked, "So why didn't you let me know you were going to be gone? Usually I see you on the weekends." *So be it if I sound like a whiny, clingy, and possessive boyfriend. I need to know. And I don't want this to happen again.*

Sam let go of Thad's hands and spread his own out in front of him in a gesture of surrender. "I am sorry. I should have called. Like I say, the trip was spur-of-the-moment, and Graziela made the arrangements. We were on a plane before I knew it. I should have thought to call you."

Yes, you should have. Thad smarted from being forgotten. How much did he mean to Sam, anyway? But what else had he said about being at the airport this morning? Had they just gotten back today?

"So what time did you get back?" Thad asked, expecting to hear a couple of hours ago.

"We got home last night. I thought about calling you, but it was late."

"I wasn't home anyway." Thad felt a little cruel saying this and couldn't deny he took pleasure in it. "But you said you were at the airport this morning..." *I wonder if I've caught him in a lie. God, I hope not. Our relationship has been going so well.*

"I was. I was." Sam paused, thinking. "We had a little trouble with my boy, Domenic." Sam chewed on his lower lip. He didn't say anything else until Thad prompted him by asking what happened.

"I don't want to bore you with the details." Sam paused again. What was going on? Was he stalling to make up a plausible story? In his mind's eye, Thad pictured Sam's handsome son behind the bar, his thick stubble, craggy face, and intense eyes.

"Bore me."

Sam waved him away. "It's okay. The family just decided Domenic might be better off going back to Sicily for a while. You know?" He switched tack...and his story. "My boy got a little homesick. That was the trouble. So we put him on a plane."

Thad cocked his head. It was on the tip of his tongue to say "I'm not quite sure I believe you. What's the real story?" but he held himself back. He didn't want to pry, and it was more than obvious Sam didn't want to talk about his son's "troubles," whatever they were. Before he had a chance to reconsider his decision, Sam spoke again.

"Listen, sweetheart, I am really behind the eight ball here. That's the correct term, right? I mean, I have a lot to do, what with being away this weekend and all. Can we get together later? Maybe you come by and have supper here tonight? I make you a big bowl of puttanesca."

Thad smiled on the outside but felt adrift at all Sam had said. He also felt he was being dismissed. "Okay, I'm not sure I'm flattered by your choice of dishes for me, but I can come by tonight." *That is, if I'm not fast asleep by six.* Thad stood and awkwardly hugged Sam. Sam patted his back, and Thad wondered if he was looking out the window to see if they had any witnesses to their display of affection.

"I can pick up a cue. It's my time to leave. I think I'll go home and take a little nap."

Sam smiled warmly...at last! "You rest up for me." He winked.

As he left the restaurant, Thad wanted to feel things had been settled, wanted to cling to Sam's final smile and promising wink, but he was troubled by all he had learned, and hadn't learned, in their brief exchange.

What bothered him most of all was why they'd sent Domenic away. And why so suddenly?

Chapter Ten

Sam heard Graziela emerge from the back just as he closed and locked the door behind Thad. The click of her heels on the hardwood stopped, and her gaze burned into his back. He wondered if she had been listening to their entire conversation. He turned to face his sister.

She was grinning at him.

"So we send Demonic away because he's 'homesick'?" Graziela laughed. "That's a good one, Sam. Why didn't you just tell your young man the truth? If he is going to be a part of your life, don't you think he should know? Don't you think he should have the, er, information he needs to decide if he wants to be with you?"

Sam put a hand to his temple. Thad's visit, all that had transpired over the weekend, and now his sister's almost accusatory words caused a sharp, needling pain behind his eyes. He closed them and moved his hands lower to press against the lids, as if he could force out the pain there. He blinked and took in his sister.

She was so beautiful, but she was a cold one. She had no heart, and the only love she had was for Sam's son. She had always been Domenic's ally and often came between father and son, undermining his paternal authority. But Sam didn't have the energy or the nerve to get into a screaming match with Graziela just now, although he knew that's probably just what she relished. So he went to the bar, poured two mugs of strong black coffee, and went to the table where only minutes ago he had sat with Thad.

Graziela frowned, but she joined him. Sam was determined to keep his voice soft and his tone even. "Look, I will tell Thad. Eventually. But you have to give me time. I want to be sure of our relationship first." Sam *was* sure of the relationship. What he was not sure of was whether telling everything about him and his family might cause Thad to run—fast—in the opposite direction. Sam wouldn't blame him.

Graziela sipped her coffee. Sam wondered how someone could look so beautiful yet be so hateful on the inside. He knew she didn't care about seeing him make a go of it with Thad. She just wanted to see the relationship destroyed. That's what she had always wanted, for them to be alone in their insulated little family. No one else allowed, unless related by blood.

"I see," she said. Sam knew she saw nothing.

"I will thank you, sister, not to take it upon yourself to reveal any family secrets to Thad. If not for me, then for Domenic and the rest of us. This is an issue that has to be handled carefully."

"I don't see why you want to fool around with that boy, anyway. Why don't you find someone like us?"

A snatch of music bubbled to the surface in Sam's thoughts, something from *West Side Story* and Anita singing to Maria about sticking to her "own kind."

"Someone Italian, you mean? A *paisano*?" Sam eyed his sister, smiling. He hoped maybe she would catch the joke and help him in lightening the tension that lay between the two of them like a live wire, sparking.

Graziela shook her head. "You know that's not what I mean. You should know, from how things went with your wife, that bringing people not like *us* into the fold can be a very dangerous thing."

A jolt of queasy nausea rocked through him at the thought of his ex-wife and all that had happened in Sicily. Domenic had never been able to forgive him. Maybe that's why he was the way he was. "You're right, sister. But I am a passionate man. We are all passionate. And I cannot help who I fall in love with." Sam wanted to add "You'd know that too, if you had ever been in love yourself" but kept quiet and reminded himself he wanted to keep things civil.

Graziela sniffed, as if she didn't believe him, as if he were making his love up as a way to irritate her. "And what of your son? Where does love come in with him? Do you think he feels love, being banished?"

Sam drew in a deep breath, reminding himself yet again to stay calm. He would not take the bait. "You know as well as I do that things were not working out here for him. He would have ruined things for us all if we let him stay. I thought we all agreed on that."

Graziela drew herself up, folding her arms across her chest. Fire sparkled in her eyes; color rose to her cheeks. When she spoke, she didn't yell, but her voice held an intensity that would have made screaming a much better option. "We all *agreed*, as you put it, because of the alternative." Tears rose to his sister's eyes. "I can't believe you could do that...to your own son." Graziela stared down and whispered, "Just because he doesn't accept you for what you are."

Sam felt sick at the thought of what he had originally proposed for Domenic. Didn't Graziela realize it broke his heart too? And in his defense, he didn't know if he could have gone through with the plan he had originally proposed.

Yes, they were werewolves. But they were also Italian. And with Italians, family always came first. That was the reason he had sent Domenic away, back to the place from which they had all come. Maybe back there, amidst the rocky outcroppings and the olive trees, Domenic could learn to behave.

And learn to love his father.

Sam looked up at his sister, feeling his own eyes sting with tears. "I'm sorry, but I can't talk about this anymore. What's done is done."

Graziela sneered. "Yes. Indeed." She crossed the room to pick up the morning paper, holding it aloft so Sam could read its werewolf headline from across the room. "What's done is done."

*

As Thad approached his door, he heard the familiar tone from his cell phone signaling he had a text message waiting. He paused to extract the phone from his pocket and read.

Can I see you? I don't like being by myself.

Thad sighed. Jared.

He couldn't blame his friend for not wanting to be alone. The poor guy had been through horror and trauma beyond Thad's understanding and wildest imaginings. But Thad was tired...and that was the plain and simple truth of it. He knew he should be a better friend. He knew he should reach right down into some bottomless reservoir of sympathy and be there for Jared, but his energy needle sat firmly on Empty. All he could think about right now was taking Edith out to do her business, coming back inside, stripping off his clothes, and collapsing onto the bed for a long nap—perhaps one that would last until the next morning.

He unlocked the door and smiled in spite of his weariness as Edith jumped at his shins, yapping and bouncing as though her legs were equipped with springs. "Okay, okay." He took the dog outside and called Jared. It was easier to talk than text when you had a fiery Mexican dog at the end of a leash, pulling you every which way.

Jared sounded tired himself when he answered.

"How are you? Are you feeling any better?" Thad did his best to put his exhaustion aside, to demonstrate his concern for his troubled friend.

"I'm scared." Jared's voice was whispery, unlike the voice he used to know. The one that cracked wise, that was full of sexual innuendo, that could always make Thad laugh. Thad missed that voice. "And I can't sleep. Can you believe it? I am too tired to sleep."

Thad did laugh at that. He couldn't help it. He understood and empathized only too well with that particular plight. "I know. I know exactly what you mean. I feel the same. Listen, I was about to go in and take a nap. I just had a weird talk with Sam, and I'm so tired I can barely stand up."

"I'm sorry. I shouldn't have bothered you."

"You know that's not what I mean!"

"What did you mean, then?"

"I only meant I need to sleep. Just like you do." Thad had an idea. "Don't take this the wrong way, but if you feel up to it, why don't you come on over on your bike? We can nap together. Maybe it'll help us both to sleep with a warm body close by." Thad realized that, in other times, this would have been just what Jared wanted to hear. Under almost any other circumstances, his words could not be interpreted in any other way than seductive.

"I know what would really help me get to sleep..." Jared's voice took on some of its old suggestive qualities, and Thad smiled. His friend hadn't completely taken leave of his old self. But Thad was pretty sure he had willpower enough if Jared did attempt to make a move on him, even next to him in bed, that he could stave him off.

Maybe.

"I'm happy to hear your mind hasn't completely vacated the gutter."

And it was so good, then, to hear Jared laugh.

"Sure. I'll come over. I've been waiting since the first day I met you to get an invite into your bed. No matter how bad I feel, there is no fuckin' way I'm turning down this offer. Later!" And Jared broke the connection.

Thad wanted to tell him that he'd leave the door open, that Jared should feel free to come inside and just crawl into bed with him. He would have to trust that Jared could figure things out for himself. He wasn't sure he could keep his eyes open long enough to wait for Jared to make the short trip to his apartment. He just didn't know what he'd wake up to or if he was opening a door that might not be able to be closed.

Inside, he unleashed Edith, freshened up her water bowl, and took off his running clothes. He sniffed at his pits to make sure he didn't smell too heinous after his run—the thought of even a shower was daunting—decided he didn't, and stripped, leaving his sweaty shorts, shirt, and socks in a heap on the floor. He slid into a pair of worn gray sweats and an old oversized T-shirt and crawled into bed. Aiming the remote at the TV, he turned it on and was pleased the see an old rerun of *The Golden Girls*. The show was television comfort food to him, and before Blanche had made even one lascivious comment, Sophia cracked wise, or Dorothy given one of her classic deadpan double-takes, he had drifted off to sleep.

*

Thad ran, the silvery course before him lit by the moon. His legs felt strong as they pounded the wooded trail, and he breathed easily. The night air cooled the sweat on his body, and it occurred to him that he should run at night more often. He looked down at his feet and saw they were bare, yet he felt no pain as he dashed over pebbles, earth, and pine needles.

And then he realized something else: his feet were not the only things bare. He wore nothing. Yet as he gazed down at his naked body, at his dick bobbing up and down with his steady rhythm, he couldn't believe how good he felt and thought maybe running nude at night should be his normal routine going forward. His breath came in and out of his lungs effortlessly, and his legs felt as though they could go for miles and miles without tiring.

A scream pierced the darkness, and Thad's good feelings dashed away from him like traitors. He stopped in the woods, listening for the pained anguish of the man's cry once more. He heard nothing save for the wind, now stronger, rustling the leaves in the trees. The moon disappeared behind a bank of clouds, and Thad realized he wasn't alone.

Someone, very close by, watched him.

"Who's there?" Thad cried into the shadows.

The wind answered him, telling him nothing.

A twig snapped, and something with a heavy tread approached. Thad's temperature dropped as the thing in the woods drew nearer. He peered into the darkness, frozen, both dreading and anticipating what he would soon see emerge if the thing stayed true to its course. He stopped breathing. The sound of his hammering heart was suddenly all he could hear.

A branch moved and the interloper revealed himself. Sam.

He was naked too. His hair-covered muscular body glistened in the moonlight with sweat, much like Thad's own. An almost painful-looking erection jutted out before him, impossibly hard. It leaked precum onto the ground below.

"Mio amore," Sam whispered, raising his arms.

Thad closed his eyes, giddy with passion, the residue of fear, and relief. He went to Sam and found himself engulfed in the man's strong embrace. Sam pulled him against his own body so tightly it just about cut off Thad's wind. But he wouldn't have stopped him. He buried his face in Sam's stubbled neck, inhaling and kissing. He smelled sweat and something else, something foreign, with a sharp metallic tang. His mind flashed briefly on the scream he had heard only moments before. But his rising cock and wildly elevating internal temperature forced the fear out of his mind, to be replaced by a hunger so overwhelming Thad could only pause for a second to marvel at the uniqueness of it.

And then their mouths mashed together, hard, tongues dueling, and Sam reached down to play with Thad's aching cock, bringing him close to release with his deft fingers. But that would have been too soon.

Sam spun him around and, with a strong hand, forced Thad to bend over. Sam positioned himself at Thad's hole and pushed savagely inside. Thad cried out as white-hot needles of pain coursed through him. But they vanished almost immediately, and he found himself pushing backward into Sam's frenzied thrusts, hoping to get him inside deeper, deeper...

Sam rode him faster, and Thad reveled in the sound of his lover's breath quickening. He knew Sam would come soon, and he couldn't wait to be filled with his seed. He reached back to pull at Sam's thighs, urging him in as deeply as possible so his gut was mashed against Thad's cheeks. He wanted to feel the pulse of Sam's dick as he exploded deep within him.

"Mio Dio!" Sam shouted into the darkness, bucking, writhing, and groaning. He pounded even harder into Thad, emptying his seed. At the same time, Thad looked down to his own cum jetting out, pale and ghostly in the moonlight, shooting three feet or more in ever-decreasing ebbs. It felt like the very life was being drained from him.

It felt wonderful.

He stood slowly and let Sam's cock slip from his hole. Finally, with a small pop, the head slapped against Thad's thigh, wet. Thad closed his eyes, trying to calm his beating heart and accelerated breathing. "That was amazing." He stood up fully and turned to kiss Sam.

Behind him stood an all-black creature, a giant wolf, standing on its hind legs. Its eyes blazed, and it panted, its tongue lolling out of its mouth and revealing a row of fangs coated in blood.

*

Thad threw himself away from the hands grabbing him. A strangled scream still burned in his throat. He practically fell from his bed, trying desperately to get away from the claws attempting to grab at him and hold him down. He batted at whoever was on him, punching and slapping.

"Hey! Hey! Stop! You had a bad dream, that's all. It's just me."

Thad finally opened his eyes and looked up into Jared's concerned gaze. He held Thad's hands back by his wrists, his face twisted into an expression of sympathy and, yes, fear. "It's okay now. It was just a dream."

Thad looked around his little studio as if seeing it for the first time. Edith sat at the edge of the bed, watching him. The TV—now playing a rerun of *Roseanne*—squawked softly. Pale gray light outside told him it was late afternoon. He forced himself to breathe regularly and to swallow.

He looked again at Jared, who now smiled kindly at him.

"Honey...you must have been having one hell of a nightmare." Jared let go of Thad's wrists and drew him close to his bare chest. "I'm sorry if I made it any worse."

Thad still couldn't find the presence of mind to form words. He simply buried his face in Jared's chest, comforted by the feel of his friend's strong hands stroking his hair and soothing him.

"I just let myself in. I hope that's okay. The door was unlocked. You were dead to the world, man, so I took the liberty of just climbing in with you. Your snores knocked me out." Jared stopped stroking Thad's hair. "Until your screaming woke me up."

Thad moved away and locked gazes with Jared. "Sorry."

"No. No, it's okay. I'm glad I was here."

Thad let himself recline on his pillow once more, and Jared did the same, both on their backs. "For a while,"

Jared said, "it was kind of hot. You were moaning, and it definitely didn't sound like a nightmare." He chuckled. "You were pushing your ass up against my crotch."

Thad reddened. "Are you naked?"

"Nah. I have my boxers on. But much more of those moves, and I gotta tell you, I might have taken 'em off, sleep or no sleep. There's only so much a man can withstand."

Thad thought the appropriate response right now would be to laugh, but the remains of the nightmare still clung to him, like clammy hands trying to pull him back down. "Jesus."

"And then there was a shift. You tightened up and the screaming started."

"Thank you for being here, buddy." Thad turned to look at Jared.

"No prob. What was the dream about, anyway?"

Thad closed his eyes and the dream images rose up to assault him. He hoped they would disappear quickly, but right now he felt as though they would stay with him for a long, long time. "I don't want to talk about it."

Chapter Eleven

Thad faced Sam across the checkered tablecloth. At the Blue Moon Café, the diners had trickled down to a dedicated few, lingering over almond biscotti and *vino santo* or a final grappa. Between them lay a great tray of imported Italian cheeses, clusters of grapes, perfect tangerines, and a bowl filled with hazelnuts and walnuts, still in their shells. A nutcracker lay close by, ready to be pressed into service.

Yet most of this postdinner feast sat untouched. The espresso Sam had insisted on them having had gone cold.

Thad had eaten little that night, in spite of Sam trying to tempt him with a black truffle risotto and sautéed Swiss chard with garlic, olive oil, and a dusting of fresh nutmeg.

Sam looked into Thad's eyes and covered Thad's hands with his own. "What's the matter? You have been cold and distant all night. I try to make you happy. Try and tempt you with my cooking, with me, and yet it's like you're not you anymore, if that makes any sense."

It wasn't fair to be so chilly with Sam. He had done nothing wrong, not really. But Thad couldn't help the feelings that clustered and festered inside him, mostly residue from his nightmare earlier that day, but also from the plague of doubt that had arisen after Sam had told him about his weekend *full-moon* trip to New York. A trip of which Sam could have easily given him a little advance notice. There was also the fact that Sam had sent his son back to Sicily, hurriedly and one might say secretively, under the remnants of a *full moon*.

Part of Thad wanted to giggle at the thoughts and suspicions clouding his thinking. *Werewolves? Really? Aren't they the stuff of legend? Is it even remotely reasonable—or sane—to give Jared's description of the wolfman creature he said he had seen any credence? Couldn't Jared just have been in shock and his own memory conjured up something fantastic and chilling? Stranger things have happened. But there's little stranger than the idea of a werewolf roaming the streets and parks of a major city like Seattle. It seems absurd.*

But is it?

"I hope you can at least put aside this difference enough to sleep with me tonight." Sam smiled, but Thad caught a bit of apprehension behind the smile, as if Sam were no longer confident in Thad's response to the idea. Thad had been so immersed in doubt and fear, enough to make his stomach churn, that he had sort of drifted away from Sam, even though he remained physically seated at this old oak table with him.

He looked up at the man he thought he loved and recoiled. Could he sleep with him tonight? The idea, one that had once held so much promise and passion, now filled him with a queasy kind of dread. Thad bit at his lip and was seized with an almost irresistible urge to cry...with loss and regret.

I really thought I was falling in love with Sam. He's my dream come true. My Mr. Right. How could all that just fly out the window with a few doubts, doubts even I think border on the lunatic?

Thad fingered the linen of the tablecloth, not allowing himself to look up at Sam as he pondered the origin of the word lunatic: *luna*, as in moon.

It all comes back to the same thing, doesn't it? Why not just put my fears on the table? Why not just ask the things I'm burning to know? Maybe if I do that, I can clear the air, repair the break in the bridge between me and the man I thought I loved?

Because if I do that, Sam will think I'm crazy, and he'll reject me.

Because if I do that, Sam will tell me the truth—he and his whole family are homicidal werewolves—and then what will I do with that?

Because if I do that, Sam will laugh at my fears and then follow me home and murder me to ensure I do not reveal the secret of the Italian family in Seattle.

Thad laughed out loud, inappropriately and maybe in something a bit too close to a hysterical twitter, and then stopped. He looked up at Sam and a combustible mixture of feelings pulsed through him within only a second or two: lust, loss, desire, regret, horror, passion, and doubt chief among them.

"Talk to me," Sam commanded, his dark eyes clouded with what looked a lot like worry to Thad.

What if this is all in my head? What if Sam really is just a humble chef who wants to make a success of his restaurant? What if he's just a guy who loves and lusts after me?

Sam went on, "You have been distant all night. I don't know what's wrong unless you tell me."

And there, poised on the brink, Thad almost did. He nearly poured out all his half-gelled fears and wants. He was close to telling Sam he wanted to put things back to where they were before their most recent full moon.

Yet he didn't know if he could. He stood suddenly, startling Sam. "I have a lot going on in my head, as you've noticed." Thad found he was trembling and, once again, on the brink of tears. He crossed to where Sam sat, stooped, and planted a deep kiss on his lips, not caring who saw. He pulled away, searching Sam's eyes and wishing he could make him understand. "I think I love you, Sam, but I'm not sure—right now—if I love *you* or the *idea* of you. I don't know if that makes sense. I don't know if any of what I'm thinking makes sense. I just know I need time to sort it all out."

Thad forced himself to turn away and scurry from the restaurant. He didn't stop, even when he heard the door reopen and Sam call after to him to come back.

"Thad, please!" Sam's voice caught at him as surely as if the man had run up behind him and grabbed at his jacket. He stopped for a moment, indecisive.

Then he continued on, shoulders hunched against a cold night wind that blew across the lake's water. Sudden drizzle stung his face, and as Thad hurried away, Sam's plaintive voice echoing behind him, the rain came down harder, soaking him. Thad looked around, at the lights in the windows of houses, warm, and the traffic rushing by him. He suddenly felt something he had not felt in a long time.

Alone.

But what really had changed? Could a nightmare and some outlandish suspicions actually thwart what he thought was the start of a promising relationship?

It wasn't Sam. It couldn't be Sam. A man so full of love and life, so full of nurturing, could not be a killer. I could not have slept with a killer. I could not have let a killer make love to me. Things like that happen to other people, people you read about in those true crime books or see on TV shows. I am not a victim.

And Sam is not a victimizer. Sure, in bed he can be rough, but it's always at my behest.

Thad paused there in the rain to think about their lovemaking, which was anything but gentle. It was often hard and ruthless, full of not nips but bites, nipples twisted beyond pleasure into pain, punches to the chest that left marks...

And I loved it all. Sam knows it. He wouldn't go there if I hadn't shown him how much I loved it. For Christ's sake, rough sex does not make the guy a killer—or a werewolf.

That's ridiculous.

But as Thad walked on through the night and the downpour, he slowed his pace. He was already soaked; a few more drops would make no difference. He began thinking about something that had nagged at him since early this morning...Domenic, Sam's son. He pictured the young man in his mind's eye: the handsome countenance, chiseled and stubbled, like out of some tough-guy thug porno. He considered Domenic's powerful shoulders, the biceps that tested the endurance of his always-black T-shirts, and the way he seldom smiled. The look could be alluring, surly and sexy, but it could also be viewed as cruel.

Why had Sam sent his own son away so quickly, almost as if he were rushing him out of the country?

Thad stopped in the shadows, his heart thudding. Did Domenic know something about his father? Something that could destroy the man? Was that why he had been banished back to the old country?

Stop it. These thoughts are lunacy.

There's that word again! I need to talk to Sam and maybe even lay out my fears, ridiculous as they may be.

If I don't, any chance the two of us might have to make good on what was a very promising beginning could be lost.

Is that what I want?

*

Thad opened his door to find Jared on his love seat with Edith curled up beside him, as if she didn't even notice Thad had left. Thad stared at the back of Jared's blond head, at the TV on in front of him, playing an episode of *Top Chef*, at a bowl of freshly popped corn on the coffee table and a glass of Coke sitting next to it.

The scene was so homey and domestic that Thad wondered if he had stepped into the wrong apartment, if indeed he had stepped into the wrong life. It suddenly seemed as though his life were an episode of *Twilight Zone* with the premise that he had never existed at all, and that a young blond man named Jared lived in his studio, owned his dog, slept in his bed... And Jared had never heard of Thad.

But then Jared must have heard him come in, because he turned and smiled at Thad. "The show's just starting. I can pause it while you get comfy. There's enough popcorn here for two. That is if you're not too full of all that eye-talian crap. I just took Edith out, so you can relax."

Thad stood still at the door, not sure how he felt about Jared making himself so at home. On one hand it was comforting to come in after an awkward and confusing night with someone you thought you loved and find another someone waiting for you. Jared was simple and uncomplicated. He made Thad laugh. He was close to his own age, and in spite of Thad's passionate entanglement with Sam, Jared was sexy as hell. There was a kind of warmth to having Jared here, almost as if they were a couple who had lived together for a long time.

On the other hand Thad wondered, as he grabbed some sweats and a flannel shirt from his dresser and headed into the bathroom to discreetly change, if he wouldn't have just preferred to have come back and found the apartment empty. Part of him simply wanted the time alone to be depressed, to be angry, to sulk, to lick at his wounds. That part wanted solitary time to think about Sam, to decide if his fears were irrational and if he needed to rudely push them aside so his romance with this hot man could continue onward, unabated.

Part of him wanted Edith to himself! Jared had his own dogs, anyway. And who the hell was looking after them at the moment?

But there was little he could do right now but accept the fact that Jared had made the decision to stay, even though Thad had assumed he would have gone back to his own place while Thad was having dinner with Sam. He understood. Jared was probably still afraid of being alone. Who wouldn't be? And Thad knew he should have the selfless heart to welcome his friend into his home, even if it was for another night, or even a few days, so he could calm down and let the horrific memories fade a bit before he faced time alone.

So he plopped down on the couch next to Jared and grabbed a handful of popcorn from the bowl. Their thighs touched. Jared aimed the remote at the TV and started *Top Chef* going again. "It's the Quick Fire Challenge," he said.

"Cool." Thad leaned back into the couch, patted Edith's head, and let his own head slide onto Jared's shoulder.

Chapter Twelve

Thad awakened the next morning to the sound of rain drumming against his window. Even though the alarm clock on his bedside table read a quarter after nine, it still appeared almost as dark as night outside. The wind howled. A low-hanging branch banged intermittently against his front window. The bed, pillow, and covers were a warm cocoon.

He felt safe, secure. He was still too drowsy to think of his awkward meeting with Sam the night before and his troubling thoughts about the man and his family. Right now he simply felt warm, snuggled down under his comforter, the body-heated pillows bunched beneath his head. In seconds, he knew, he could drift right back into a deep slumber.

An arm went over his shoulder, and he felt a warm body press against his back. Thad closed his eyes, guilty for not first imagining the body pressed up against him was Sam's. It was Jared's. In addition to the warmth radiating from Jared's body, an insistent erection also poked at the back of Thad's boxers.

Thad didn't move away. Yet he wasn't sure what he should do once he felt Jared begin to thrust against his backside. Should he reach down and pull off his boxers, let nature take its course?

In spite of his feelings and doubts about Sam, he simply couldn't travel that road. Things were still too unsettled between them. Thad was a one-man man, always had been. And he could tell, from Jared's even breathing just a degree north of a snore, that he still slept and wasn't putting the moves on Thad.

So Thad grabbed his friend's hand and pulled it off him, then turned to lie flat on his back, positioning himself so Jared would be forced to move away. He glanced over at Jared, still asleep, blond hair askew against the pillow, the pale brown stubble on his face, the slightly parted Cupid's-bow lips that caused a nearly irresistible urge in Thad to plant a lingering kiss on them.

Where would be the harm?

The harm would be that it would just add more confusion to the mix, and Thad was already mixed up enough as it was. The sight of Jared turning his head toward him, licking his lips, and opening his eyes to stare at him interrupted Thad's thoughts. Jared's eyes were the bluest he had ever seen. So different from Sam's.

Jared reached over and stroked Thad's face for a minute, smiling. "I was dreaming about you." His voice was husky from sleep.

"I know."

"You do?"

"Never mind." Thad made himself scoot over so Jared's hand fell away from his face. The touch was making his own dick harden, in spite of his best intentions. And his dick had been known to pull a demonic possession routine on him in the past, and he needed to stay strong.

"Do I have morning breath?" Jared asked. He stretched and lowered the comforter so his arms and part of his chest emerged. Thad couldn't help but notice the downy pale brown hair that coated his friend's forearms and his smooth, muscled chest.

So unlike Sam.

"We both do, so don't worry about it. Did you sleep okay?"

"Mmmm... Thanks for letting me crash here. Don't worry. I can probably head back today. I have things to do, dogs to take care of...and messes, I am so sure, to clean up. I also eventually have to go to work. And I have to be by myself sometime."

Thad was surprised by the twinge of sadness that went through him as he contemplated Jared leaving. But what else would he do? They were just pals, right? Jared couldn't exactly stay there forever. Could he?

Why not? Forget about Sam. Maybe Edith would enjoy the company of Jared's dogs; they could be like siblings to her.

The thought rose up almost like another voice in his head. Thad told it to hush. "You take your time. I don't mind you being here."

Jared reached down and squeezed Thad's cock.

"I can tell." He laughed, and Thad was confronted by two conflicting emotions: lust and betrayal. The former from down below, the latter from his head.

He elbowed Jared's hand away. "Behave, you!" To cut off the direction things were heading, Thad sat up. "I need to take Edith out, and then I'll make us some coffee."

"Will you bring it to me in bed? On a tray with two pieces of lightly buttered toast and a couple soft-boiled eggs?" Jared batted his eyelashes, grinning.

"Don't press your luck, buddy. In fact, since I am going to be braving the rain outside with Edith, why don't *you* make the coffee?" Thad stood and struggled into the sweats and shirt from the night before. "Beans are in the freezer, grinder in the cupboard above that. You know where the pot is."

"You're no fun." Jared got up from bed. His body was graceful, defined, and his plaid boxers tented outward with his morning wood. Thad questioned his sanity in turning away this offering.

Edith hopped impatiently against his leg. He looked down at her as if she knew what she was interrupting and was doing it for Thad's own good. "Thanks, sweetie." He scooped her up and went over to the door, where her leash and collar hung on a hook. "Be back in a few."

"Okay." Jared trotted into the bathroom and closed the door behind him. Before Thad could get outside, he could hear the rush of pee hitting against the water in the bowl.

When he got back, Thad smelled the coffee brewing. Again he was struck by how homey and domestic things seemed with Jared there. Jared had already found two mismatched mugs from his cupboard and set them out on the breakfast bar, along with the pint carton of half-and-half from the fridge and the canister of sugar from his counter. He had pulled off some paper towels from the roll above the sink and put out two spoons. A pot of water boiled on the stove, the egg carton beside it, and bread sat in the toaster.

One thing Thad could say about Jared was that he was not pretentious.

But he was thoughtful.

"You makin' us some breakfast? You didn't have to do that."

"Soft-boiled eggs and toast isn't exactly hard. Dry your hair off and grab a stool. This will be ready in..." Jared stopped talking long enough to lower four eggs into the boiling pot and push the bread down in the toaster. "Four minutes."

Soon the remains of their breakfast—yolks, bits of egg white, and bread crusts—sat before them. Thad set his plate on the floor so Edith could lick up the remains of the egg. When she finished, he held the plate up to Jared. "All clean. Just put it back in the cupboard." The plate did sparkle. And Jared smiled.

"We need to talk."

"Oh?"

"Yeah. I've been thinking this whole time that maybe you and I need to find out what's going on here, play a little detective, if you will. We need to do this so another gay dude in Seattle doesn't get ripped to shreds. Especially when the dude could be one of us."

Uneasily, a thought rose in Thad's mind, borne up by his subconscious. He hadn't considered it before, but now it made perfect sense...and it caused a shiver to course through him. *The problem's been taken care of. It's been sent back to Italy.* But he didn't say that. He realized that if doing something proactive like this would help Jared conquer his fears, then he would be happy to do it. "So where were you thinking we should start?"

"Good question. Do you remember that killing last September? In the Arboretum?"

Thad nodded and sipped at his coffee, which had now gone tepid.

"Well, if you recall, I am not the only one who witnessed a killing. The news reports at the time said there were some other guys who saw what happened, or at least had a glimpse."

"Yeah, I remember that. But it also said something like they couldn't recall much of what they had seen. It was dark and over so fast."

"Right. That's what the papers reported. But maybe they were like me. Maybe they were too afraid to talk about it. Maybe, like me, they were too afraid of the images in their own minds to give them any credence."

"You could be right about that." Thad got up to pour himself a fresh cup of coffee. He held up the pot to Jared and raised his eyebrows.

Jared shook his head. "Another cup will put me on the toilet for the next two hours."

"Lovely."

"Get over it. While you were at dinner last night, I managed to call a reporter from one of the papers. You know, that alternative weekly? Anyway, it took me a few times with a few different folks, but eventually I was able to get the names of the witnesses."

"Really?" Thad sat back down with his coffee. He was surprised it had been that easy.

"Yeah, I thought there would be some problems with confidentiality, shit like that, but I guess their names were a matter of public record. It just took me talking to the right person to get the info." Jared raised his eyebrows. "As you know, I can be very persuasive."

Entirely unbidden came the memory of Jared getting out of bed that morning, his erection tenting out the front of his boxers. It gave Thad a not entirely unpleasant jolt. "I know," he said, voice a little hoarse.

Jared stood and crossed the room. He fished in his jeans pocket and pulled out a folded yellow Post-it note. He held it up. "Three names. One in Wallingford and the other two on the Hill. I say we go talk to them today."

"But do you have their information? Surely the paper didn't give you their addresses and phone numbers?"

"No, but the Internet did. You in?"

"Sure. I just have to take a shower and we can go."

As Thad headed off to the bathroom, he wasn't sure at all they were doing the right thing. He didn't quite understand his feelings, since the plan made sense. It might not only give Jared some peace, but it might also lead to apprehending the killer, if the witnesses could pull their impressions together coherently enough.

But who was the killer? And did Thad really want him exposed?

Some things we are better off not knowing.

Thad locked the bathroom door and stripped, turned on the hot water in the shower as hard as he could stand it, and stepped inside, luxuriating in the spray. He didn't want to think anymore.

Chapter Thirteen

Thad and Jared had no luck on Capitol Hill.

They'd been able to call upon both witnesses living there, one an overweight, pale young man who looked terrified of them, and the other a painfully thin guy with a buzz cut, nose piercing, bad teeth, and reddish sores on his face and arms. Thad thought the latter looked like—and probably was—a crystal meth addict. Both men were receptive enough to Thad and Jared, although the suspected meth addict would not let them inside his apartment, preferring to talk to them from a partially opened front door.

Both had the same story. They'd told everything they knew to both the police and the press. What they knew was this—they'd only seen a blur of motion through the dark, which could have been anything, a person or a beast. The overweight guy said that it could even have been something paranormal, a black ghost. "It moved so fast, it was scary," he whispered, his eyes growing large.

Thad wondered if he remembered more than he was letting on, but when he pressed for more details, the guy came up empty. "I honestly don't know what I saw." Thad didn't hold out much hope for the last person they had on their list, a James Whittier in Wallingford. Thad held fast to Jared's back as they traced a route north on his Vespa on Eastlake Avenue, heading for the Seattle neighborhood on the shores of Lake Union.

The guy who answered the door explained that it was his roommate who had come upon the crime scene and that he didn't want to talk about it anymore. "You guys reporters?" The man, older with a bald pate and oval wire-frame glasses, eyed them suspiciously. He didn't seem happy to see them.

"Nah. We're just concerned citizens." Jared gave the man his most dazzling smile, a ploy Thad had seen work its magic on any number of gay men, but it was having no effect here. Maybe the man wasn't gay but was simply a roommate, or a relative or friend, of James Whittier.

"Well, I don't think Jimmy would have much to say." The man started to close the door. "It was like the papers said. You can get that story online. You don't need to bother us at home." He looked pointedly at both Thad and Jared. "Now, if you don't mind, I have stuff to do." He closed the door in their faces.

As they were coming down the walk of the Craftsman bungalow, they saw a man, much younger, emerge from a brand-new Honda Civic hybrid. He was broad-shouldered, tan, and had long black hair. Thad imagined some Native American blood coursed through his veins.

"Woof," Jared whispered.

Thad could do little but silently agree as the man locked the car with his remote and started heading their way.

Jared was quick. "Excuse me." He smiled and planted himself in front of the raven-haired man. "Are you James Whittier?"

The man smiled, looking Jared up and down and then taking in Thad. His gray eyes seemed to sparkle. "I could be. Who wants to know?"

"I'm Jared, and this is my friend, Thad."

"Have we met before?" The man seemed amused, and Thad wondered why he would have to ask such a question.

"I don't think so," Jared said. "But if you're James Whittier, I think you and I may have something in common."

"You mean other than the fact that we're both hot?" He glanced over at Thad and hastened to add, "And your friend too?"

Thad realized all at once that maybe James thought this was some sort of come-on and that such circumstances more than likely presented themselves to him frequently. If the whole situation weren't so weird, he might have been amused. Or aroused.

"Um, yeah...other than that." Jared moved a little closer and said in a soft voice, "I think we both might have been witnesses to whoever—or whatever—is killing gay men in Seattle."

The flirtatious front immediately disappeared, and the guy's tan complexion paled. The man eyed the Craftsman house from which Thad and Jared had just come. "What do you know about that?"

"I saw it too, man." Jared's voice was soft.

"You did?" The guy seemed to debate with himself for a minute or two. "Yeah, I'm James. You can call me Jimmy. Most everyone does." He eyed the house again. "Did you go to my house?"

"Yeah, why?" Thad asked.

"Did you talk to my boyfriend?"

And now it all clicked into place for Thad. The guy at the door was this man's partner and obviously a very insecure one at that. Thad glanced back at the fine house. It was small but beautifully landscaped, and Thad was certain the upstairs windows afforded stunning views of

Lake Union and, across it, downtown Seattle. The price for a house like this would be well over a million dollars, especially in today's competitive market.

Thad took in Jimmy Whittier's studly appearance, and it all fit together: sugar daddy and pretty boy. Maybe that wasn't fair, and maybe he was jumping to conclusions, but it made sense. And what also made sense was the trouble that might have come from Jimmy being not only at the scene of a crime, but also from him wandering around in a place notorious for gay cruising.

"We talked to him," Thad said. "He didn't exactly seem receptive."

"Yeah," Jared added. "He kind of spoke for you, said you really didn't remember anything." Jared paused. "But I wonder if that's true. When I mentioned we had something in common and that it was being witnesses to a killing, I saw something in your face."

Jimmy shook his head and swallowed. "Martin doesn't really want me talking about this. Can we take a little walk? Gas Works Park is just a couple blocks over."

The men remained silent as they headed down to the park, where cold wind blew off the lake. They sat on some steps leading down to the water.

"Sorry to drag you down here." Jimmy leaned forward, angling his body so he faced both Thad and Jared. "Martin wouldn't approve if he saw me talking to you guys. I hope he didn't." He stopped for a minute and then went on. "Martin didn't like it that I was mixed up in that whole thing. Not so much that I had witnessed a murder and the trauma of that, God knows. That would have been understandable. But Martin's the jealous type, you know? He was more concerned about what I was doing in the woods at the Arboretum." Jimmy looked out at the water, his gaze pensive. "He had a pretty good idea what I was doing there. But can you blame me? He's twenty-five years older than I am." Jimmy sighed. "I just don't get what I need at home."

Thad thought this was all very interesting but not really what they had come for. "So I have to ask you. Did you see something that night?"

Jared added, "We already spoke to two of the other guys there, and they said they remembered nothing other than seeing a black shape, like a shadow, move through the trees and brush. That's pretty much what the papers said."

"Yeah, I guess the papers were right." He leaned closer to Jared and laid a hand on his thigh. Jimmy's color was high and his eyes shone. "But you saw it too, didn't you?"

Jared said nothing but nodded.

"I was too scared people would think I was crazy if I told anyone the truth. And then when Martin got so pissed off about me being out there, I figured it was best just to go along with the official version, you know? Let sleeping dogs lie. Just play along and get this thing out of our lives. I may be a bad boy, but I do love Martin."

Yeah, yeah, Thad thought. "So what *did* you see, Jimmy?"

Jimmy looked over at Jared. "He knows what I saw. Don't you?"

Jared squirmed under Jimmy's gaze. Finally he said, "I think I do. But I'd be a lot more comfortable if you said it first."

Jimmy stared out at the water again for a long time. His left arm twitched once, twice, and his face contorted with what Thad could only assume was a very painful—or very horrifying—memory.

"Okay. I saw a beast, a creature. I don't know what the fuck you'd call it."

"What did it look like, Jimmy?" Thad softly prompted.

"It looked like a big strong man and a wolf got together and had a baby...a love child from hell."

"You saw a werewolf?" Jared dug his hands into the pockets of his leather jacket. The word, spoken aloud, sounded ridiculous to Thad, as though there should be cameras, boom microphones, and a guy in a director's chair nearby.

"You didn't? What did *you* see, then?"

Jared didn't speak for several seconds, then said, "No, that's what I saw too."

Thad felt a chill course through him that had nothing to do with the autumn wind or the damp of the nearby lake. "Anything else?" he said softly, not moving his gaze away from the water's gray-blue rippled surface.

"Just the smell," Jimmy said.

"What?" Jared leaned closer to Jimmy.

"The smell. Under the blood and guts, I could smell—ah, this sounds really weird—but I could smell garlic." He said the last words in a rush. He laughed, and color rose to his cheeks.

Jared laughed too, but there was no mirth in it. "You know, I don't think I recalled that until you said it just now, but there was the strong scent of garlic in the alley that night."

A wave of nausea washed over Thad.

The three men grew quiet. Thad supposed the other two were thinking about the horror they had both witnessed. But he was thinking about the Blue Moon Café and the wonderful smells that issued forth from its kitchen. And the chief aroma wafting out of that kitchen... was garlic.

*

Thad had Jared drop him off at his apartment. The two said little as Thad dismounted from Jared's scooter. Rain began to fall steadily as the afternoon wound down into dusk. Thad didn't offer to let Jared stay another night, and he had a sense Jared was eager to get back to his own place as well. It was a good sign...wasn't it?

After taking care of Edith, Thad sat in the chair facing the TV. He didn't turn it on, nor did he turn on any lights. He watched as the shadows swallowed up the light in the room. He thought of a clichéd phrase James Whittier had used: *let sleeping dogs lie.* How fitting that he should attribute something canine to this whole situation, this mess, this beyond-belief horror extravaganza in which he suddenly found himself immersed. He didn't really want to think about any of it, but trying to train his mind on other things, or on just being still and blank for more than a few seconds, was an exercise in futility. Not thinking about the prospect of Sam and his family somehow being involved just made all the fears, suspicions, doubts, and recriminations rise up that much stronger.

He couldn't do anything more, he decided, leaning over to the switch on the floor lamp next to the chair. He reached out to the coffee table where his landline cordless lay and snatched it up.

Sam answered right away. "Blue Moon Café. This is Sam. How can I help you?"

By telling me you're not a werewolf.

By telling me your family has nothing to do with a wave of murders of gay men in Seattle that seems to coincide with your arrival here from New York.

By telling me that you love me and you already know what I'm thinking and how silly all that is. "I need to talk to you."

"I was hoping you'd call." Sam's voice was soft. "You can come over whenever you want. It's a rare slow night. I shouldn't be too busy."

"Can I come now?"

"The sooner, the better, like they say."

Thad broke the connection and went into the bathroom to finger comb his hair, splash some water on his face, and brush his teeth. He traded his beat-up flannel shirt for a black cashmere sweater, decided his jeans were clean enough, and set off.

By the time Thad reached the restaurant, the rain poured down in sheets, coating and fogging the windows of the café and making it seem warm, a sanctuary. He hurried inside to get out of the damp. When he stepped in, Graziela gave him the once-over and almost seemed amused by his drowned-rat appearance. A laugh, not quite allowed to form completely, fluttered around the edges of her red, red lips.

"I get you a towel. Sam's in the back."

She hurried away and returned with a couple of kitchen towels with which Thad began to dab at his face and hair. She left him to take up her post at the hostess desk, even though no one new had come into the restaurant.

Sam came out of the kitchen after a few minutes, drying his hands on one of the same white linen towels. His face was sweaty and his eyes were plaintive as he drank in Thad. He smiled, but it held a hint of caution Thad had never seen before. Thad wasn't sure he liked it. It was almost as though Sam were afraid of him.

Shouldn't that be the other way around, hon? If the guy's a werewolf, shouldn't I be afraid of him?

Thad shook his head, not amused with this line of thinking. "Hey."

"Hello, Thad. Do you want to sit down?" Sam led him to a table near the back of the restaurant, where it was quiet. Thad sat, and before Sam joined him, he asked, "Can I get you something to eat? I just made a big pot of *pasta fagioli*, perfect for a night like this."

"It's okay, Sam. I'm not hungry."

"Okay." Sam sat. "What did you want to talk to me about?"

Part of Thad simply wanted to tell Sam to forget it, there was really nothing he wanted to talk to him about. Part of him wanted only to say that he hoped they could find a way to just go on as they had once, with lust, blossoming love, and the promise of a shared future before them. But that prospect was impossible without first at least trying to clear up his concerns and fears.

Could he say what he needed to? Could he risk losing Sam? After all, if Thad uttered what was in his head, Sam might think he was flat-out crazy and might just humor him and then, after Thad left, tell Graziela to bar Thad admittance to the restaurant, and if Thad called, to always tell him Sam was "busy."

But it seemed there was no other way out. No other alternative than facing the truth head-on.

"You probably know, from the news anyway, that since you moved here there have been three murders in town. All gay men."

Sam cocked his head, and his dark eyes seemed to cloud, growing even darker. He nodded. Thad wanted him to say more—that he didn't know about it or to show some concern—but his silence chilled him.

Thad swallowed and wished he had more saliva in his mouth. "You know about the, er, killings, right?"

"I know. They've been on the front pages since last summer." Sam leaned close to Thad across the table, ensnaring him with his gaze. "Why you asking me about this?"

Now's the time. "I don't know. Just some weird stuff has happened. Little things...dreams, what a friend of mine saw, what another guy, James Whittier, saw at the Arboretum right after the second killing... They were both witnesses to the horrible murders. They smelled garlic at two crime scenes. You were all gone over the weekend of the full moon..." Thad's voice trailed off. Spoken aloud, it all sounded so silly, so inane, like he was in the running for the title of Scream Queen. Step aside, Miss Jamie Lee Curtis.

"And?"

How can I say this? "I don't know what to think, but I just want your assurance that you had nothing to do with any of this."

Sam's eyebrows came together with a look of concern, perhaps even alarm. And then he threw back his head and laughed so loudly and heartily that the few other diners in the restaurant stopped their conversations to stare. "So, what? Now you think I am some kind of killer? A monster? Because, why? A few nightmares? And the fact that I am not around when there is a full moon? I told you. We all went to see Nana in New York last weekend."

"I know. I know." Thad could feel heat rise to his cheeks. Out in the open like this, it all really did sound absurd.

"That looks pretty."

"What?"

"The blush in your cheeks. Makes me want to kiss you."

But one other thing rankled Thad. Before he let Sam distract him from his purpose with flattery and flirting, he had to ask. "But one other thing bothers me: Domenic."

The smile on Sam's face vanished. "What? You think Domenic is involved? I told you... We have problems. We do not always get along. We do not see eye to eye. And we are Italian. We fight. We raise our voices."

Thad nodded.

Sam snatched up Thad's hands and held them tight on the table. Sam's hands, hot, engulfed his own. "Remember when I told you, at the start, that things in my life were complicated? That maybe we shouldn't see each other? I didn't tell you then, but I should tell you now... Domenic was the reason. Not so much the restaurant and all that stuff I told you about being too busy for a relationship."

"Domenic?"

"*Sì.*"

"Why?"

"Because he does not approve of my life. Or lifestyle, as they say over here."

"You mean he has a problem with you being gay?"

Sam nodded. "Uh-huh. See, Domenic was just a little boy when his mama and I split up. There was another man, but even if there wasn't, we would have split up because I wasn't being honest with myself. You know? But in my country and in my culture, with the Catholic stuff and all that, you don't easily, how do you say it, come out? It was hard for me to finally admit to myself who I was. And then when Davio came along, it changed everything and gave me the courage to end my marriage."

Thad felt an entirely irrational flash of jealousy surge through him at the mention of another man.

"Davio and I did not work out. He was a silly queen. But he did give me the strength to live my life the way I knew I had to."

"And Domenic?"

"Domenic loves his papa. He did not want to blame me. So he looked at my being gay as something hateful, something outside of *me* instead of being part of me. That way he could hate something without hating his papa." Sam rubbed his hands over his face, petting his beard. He looked full of thought. "I wish you spoke Italian. This would be so much easier to tell you."

Thad felt a sense of relief. And the language was not a problem. He understood. Now it made so much more sense, especially the hastily convened trip to New York, probably to talk about how to solve the problem that was Domenic. Early on, Sam didn't want to see Thad, and it was most likely because he was afraid of what Domenic would think. It was probably difficult for the poor man to be trapped between two grown men, both of whom he loved.

So Sam had sent Domenic back to Sicily. Maybe it was just easier all around. Maybe Domenic wanted to go. Maybe the idea of living here in the States and watching his father with a boyfriend was intolerable.

Of course they weren't killers. Of course they weren't werewolves. Even if one *was* running around Seattle on full moon nights, it wasn't Sam or part of his family. Thad felt a laugh, borne of relief, bubble up and spring from between his lips. "I am so sorry about your trouble with Domenic."

"It's hard. But he will eventually come around."

Just then he heard shouting in the kitchen and the clatter of pans crashing to the floor. Sam looked in that direction, then back at Thad. "I will be right back."

Sam hurried away from the table. Thad rose slightly to peer over the counter that looked on the glassed-in kitchen and saw that a small grease fire had started. Staff bustled around, near hysteria, as Sam grabbed a fire extinguisher and worked on putting out the flames. The other diners in the restaurant fell to silence as they all turned their heads to take in the drama.

Thad hadn't even noticed her approach, but suddenly Graziela stood near his table. She looked down at him with her dark eyes and smiled, yet she was shaking her head. "Didn't my brother even offer you a little something to eat?"

"Oh, he did. But I wasn't hungry."

Graziela made a *tsk-tsk* sound. "Not hungry? A big, strong man like you?" Graziela snorted. "In my country, women learn to feed their men. I am gonna go back and fix you up a big bowl of *pasta fagioli* and you will eat. Okay?" For once Graziela gave him a smile that appeared to be both genuine and warm.

"Okay. I guess I have to learn you don't say no to food from an Italian."

"Especially an Italian woman. It is, how do you say it, in our genes to force food on people."

The two of them laughed, and Graziela seemed just about to move away from the table when Thad said, "I guess you got that trait from your nana."

"Oh yes, and my mama too. You want me to bring you some cheese for your *pasta fagioli*? There's lots in it already, but I like a little on top...and some olive oil too."

"That sounds wonderful." Thad found that now he had cleared the air with Sam, he actually was hungry, and the spit that had been so rare in his mouth just a few minutes ago was now back with a vengeance. "How is she, by the way?"

Graziela stopped in her course to the kitchen and turned around. She cocked her head. "How is who?"

"Your nana."

Graziela shrugged. "Okay, I guess. What makes you ask?"

"Well, you guys just visited her, right?" Thad thought he was just making conversation with Sam's sister but didn't like the look of confusion clouding her features.

"What do you mean?"

"Weren't you just out there—in New York—over the weekend?"

"No. I don't know where you got that notion. We haven't seen Nana in a long time."

It felt like someone had punched Thad in the stomach. He had to be sure. "And Sam didn't go visit?"

"No. No, of course not. Where is all this coming from?" Graziela appeared genuinely confused.

Thad wondered if the chill he felt flow through him showed on his skin, if he looked clammy and pale. "Nowhere. Never mind." *Sam lied to me. Why?* The idea of food, even the most delicious food, seemed repugnant to him now.

"I'll go get your supper, Thad."

"Never mind. I'm not so hungry anymore." The clatter and bustle in the kitchen seemed to have died down, and Thad knew Sam would be returning to the table any minute. He didn't know if he could face him, not without flying into a rage or bursting into tears.

If he wasn't in New York, where was he? Where were all of them?

He thought of asking Graziela but didn't feel comfortable with that idea. He just wanted, more than anything, to get out of the Blue Moon Café so he could breathe once more and lick his wounds.

Graziela laughed, obviously not spotting the terror on his face. "What did I just tell you, young man? You are eating!" And she started off toward the kitchen.

Thad called after her. "Graziela!"

"Yes?" She looked back at him, over her shoulder.

"Where's Domenic?"

Her expression clouded over. "What do you know about that?"

"Sam just said he went back to Sicily." Was that too a lie?

"Well then, you already know where Domenic is." Graziela hurried off to the kitchen.

And Thad hurried out the door—into the night, into the rain, into a world unencumbered with lies, doubts, and misgivings. At least until he got home.

What was going on?

Chapter Fourteen

NOVEMBER

"So I haven't seen him since that night. I miss him so much, but I just don't know that I can abide a liar. I don't know what the fuck's going on."

Thad took a sip of his dirty martini, his third of the night, and looked over at Jared, perched on the barstool next to him. They were at the Cell, a dark and once-smoky leather bar on Pine Street. The place had gritty hardwood floors, Colt and Tom of Finland posters on the walls, and a St. Andrew's cross in one corner. Techno music played softly from the bar's stereo system. Video monitors played endless loops of soft-core leather porn. Jared had called Thad earlier and announced that he was ready to go out again. The poor thing had not been inside a bar since the fateful night he'd seen his latest trick being literally devoured by a monster. Jared had also not seen a man naked since that night. It was beginning to get on his nerves.

Thad was only too glad to join him. Ever since he had discovered that Sam had lied about his weekend away from him, he didn't know what to do. It had turned what he thought had been a relationship with a lot of promise on its head. Yet Thad could not shut his feelings off like a spigot simply because they were inconvenient. He still thought of Sam in loving and lustful terms.

And then he would think of how Sam had told him, in detail, of the family trip to New York...*a trip that had never happened*. Confusion and doubt shadowed everything Thad had thought to be true. He wondered what else Sam had lied to him about.

Of course, Sam had tried to make it up to him. He had called, he had sent flowers, a basket of anise-scented biscotti, and a bottle of *vino santo*. Hell, he had even shown up on Thad's doorstep more than once, begging forgiveness.

And Thad would have forgiven him, if Sam had only come clean. But the closest thing he could get to an explanation from Sam was that there were things he couldn't talk about with him, not yet. But he promised that, in due time, he would explain everything to Thad.

In due time?

That wasn't good enough.

So Thad remained in limbo. His feelings for Sam prevented him from moving on, from making a break, from seeing other men. But at the same time, he wasn't sure what he was doing. Was he in a relationship or not?

So when the old Jared had called earlier tonight, full of good cheer, horniness, and humor, Thad knew his friend could provide an evening of oblivion. And oblivion was just what he needed.

The funny thing was, right after he hung up from Jared, the phone had rung again. Thad didn't bother to look down at the Caller ID, assuming it would just be Jared calling back to tell him something he'd forgotten, something along the lines of which color jockstrap he should wear under his faded and ripped Levi's.

"Clutter's Fish Market," Thad had answered the phone.

"What?"

Sam's voice had surprised him. He looked down at the Caller ID too late and saw Samuel Lupino there in digital letters. If he had only looked before he picked up, he could have saved himself from more of the same awkwardness he'd been doing his best to avoid all month. He was annoyed that Sam was calling; couldn't he just leave him alone to think? He didn't really want to talk to him until the man was ready to tell the truth. A cold, irrational anger coursed through Thad. Jared had finally succeeded in putting him in a good mood, and Thad at last was looking forward to an evening where he wouldn't agonize about Sam, and here was Sam, already spoiling it.

"Nothing. It was a joke. A dumb one. Have you called to finally tell me what's going on with that weird family of yours? With that weird man I thought I knew? You know, the one called Sam? *If* that *is* your real name..."

"You're not being fair."

"No, *you're* not being fair. If you want to lie to me and you don't want to let me fully into your life, I don't see how we can build a future together. We need trust...and right now, Sam, I just don't have any. You should understand that." Thad longingly eyed the jeans and long-sleeved black T-shirt he had laid out on his bed.

Don't spoil this for me. Just don't. I don't know where you and I are headed, but that's the last thing I want to think about tonight.

"I will tell you everything...soon. I love you, Thad."

The statement just made Thad more furious. If Sam loved him, why play these games? Thad needed to end this conversation. "Listen, I have plans tonight."

"Oh? A man?"

Thad considered for a moment explaining that his plans were simply with a friend and there was nothing between them. But why should he? Sam had obviously been less than honest with him, and maybe a little jealousy would force his Italian man to be a little more forthcoming. So Thad said, "Yes. A man. I mentioned him before. Jared?"

Sam didn't say anything for a long while. To fill the silence, Thad said, "I met him through my volunteer work. We're meeting up at his place on Capitol Hill."

"Do I know him?"

Thad felt almost cruel. It was both a victorious feeling and one that filled him with regret. He heard the hurt in Sam's voice, even though he wasn't there with him. Thad almost relented, but instead, he twisted the knife. "Jared Holmes? He gets around, so maybe you do know him? Lives on Aloha?"

"You have fun." Sam's voice and tone were chilly.

And Thad couldn't bear it. "Look, if you'll see me tonight...and lay all your cards on the table, I'll cancel my date. Fair enough?"

Sam was silent for a long time. "I can't. I have plans tonight."

"What are you doing?"

"Just some family stuff. I will be out of town."

"What are you doing, Sam? Tell me." Thad felt himself begin to tremble, and a queasy nausea rose up in his gut.

"We can talk later. How about tomorrow?"

"Why not tonight?" Thad pressed.

"Tonight is no good. I have to go." And Sam broke their connection.

Thad had to fight to resist the impulse to call him back. In the end, he decided to prime the pump and poured himself a large glass of vodka while he turned the shower on, setting it to steaming hot. He hoped he could find his way back to careless abandon and oblivion.

Men!

So now here he sat with Jared, and what were they talking about? Sam. Thad signaled the bartender for another martini, and Jared looked at him in surprise. "You better watch yourself there, pardner. I'm not sure I'm strong enough to carry you out of here."

"Look, I just want to have some fun. Okay?" Thad handed the bartender a ten when he set down yet another chilled glass before him. "Keep the change, sweet cheeks."

After the bartender wandered away, Jared asked, "Sweet cheeks? That does not sound like you."

"Well, maybe I don't want to be me tonight." Thad looked around the bar, which had filled with more and more men as the evening wore on. The best way to distract Jared from Thad's troubles was to divert his attention to Jared's favorite subject: hot men.

"See anything you like?"

Jared's gaze roamed the place, and when his expressionless features twisted into a lopsided grin, Thad knew the answer to his question. Jared had obviously spotted a good prospect. Thad swiveled in his barstool to see upon whom Jared's gaze had lit.

Across the bar, someone stood out from the crowd of leather daddies, bears, and less noticeable guys in their flannel shirts, Cons, and jeans. A tall African-American man leaned against the wall near the door, holding a bottle of Budweiser in one hand and coolly surveying the crowd. He wore baggy jeans that rode low on his hips, construction worker boots, a white V-neck muscle shirt that showed off a broad expanse of smooth and defined chest upon which lay a large gold chain, and a beat-up black hoodie zippered sweatshirt with a skull design. The guy had a shaved head, gold hoops in each ear, and a chinstrap beard that was so expertly trimmed it reminded Thad of topiary. Even from across the room, and even in those baggy jeans, Thad could make out a large bulge in the guy's crotch, jutting out from his impossibly smooth and flat stomach.

He reached up and turned Jared's face away from the guy. Jared was practically drooling. "Hey," Thad said. "You mean him?" He nodded toward the guy.

"Of course, him. Is there anybody else here?"

Thad grinned. "I take offense at that."

"You know what I mean. Just look at him, though. He's gorgeous. And tough. He looks dangerous. I like that in a man."

Thad wanted to tell Jared that being attracted to danger, after all he'd been through, seemed pretty hopeless. But he didn't know if he could get through the stars clouding Jared's vision. Instead he said, "He looks like a thug." And indeed he did. Complete with what looked like a gang tattoo on his neck. Thad thought neck and hand tattoos were the most hard core of all. After all, clothing couldn't hide them when they might prove inconvenient.

"I know." Jared craned to see around someone who had obstructed his view of his rough-trade ebony god. "Good Lord, he's probably a sex machine."

And before Thad knew what was happening, Jared managed to hook the guy with his blue-eyed gaze. Jared's smile was a lasso he used to reel the man over to them. Up close, the man was even more beautiful. His skin had a rich, lustrous darkness and his eyes an almost feral brownish-gold luminescence. His full lips revealed even white teeth when he smiled. Even the gold inlays in his front teeth, an affectation at which Thad would have normally scoffed, looked sexy and scary at the same time.

"Hey, I couldn't help but notice you standing over there all alone," Jared said, never once breaking eye contact with the man. "And I thought, what a shame something that hot is all by himself. And *then* I thought, what am I thinking? It's wonderful he's all alone. And then..."

To stop Jared from babbling, Thad extended his hand. "Hi, I'm Thad. And my obviously smitten friend here is Jared."

The man had an amused expression on his face as he looked over the pair of them. "TJ." He reached out to shake Thad's hand, which was when Thad noticed a small pistol in a leather holster hanging at the waistband of his baggy jeans. "Thug" was right. This guy was for real. Yet TJ's voice was warm and his smile genuine. He shook hands firmly with Thad, meeting his gaze.

Jared slid down from his stool to break the handshake, and the contact, between Thad and TJ. He maneuvered himself so his and TJ's chests were touching. "I don't care much for that handshake business. I'm all about a kiss as a way to greet new friends." And with that, he stood on tiptoe and planted a deep, lingering kiss on TJ's mouth. Over Jared's shoulder, TJ's eyes met Thad's, and Thad could read surprise, delight, and humor in the look.

Yup, the old Jared was back.

But what about the gun? Should he say something? What kind of friend would he be if he didn't? He could see, even in these few seconds, where things were headed between Jared and TJ. Jared had moved on to groping the man's crotch—so demure, so subtle! He had to say something, so he insinuated himself between the pair, much as Jared had just done. He leaned close to TJ's ear and whispered, "What's up with the gun?"

TJ stepped back and flicked his hand over the cold steel handle. Then he pulled his shirt over it and zipped his jacket closed. "You're an observant one. I could say that it's none of your business, but I can see you're concerned about your friend here."

"That's right."

"It's for protection, is all. You've heard that three guys have been killed lately? And two of 'em have been here on the Hill." TJ shrugged and put out his large hands in a gesture of surrender. "I need to take care of myself, you know? I bet I'm not the only dude packin' these days. Can you blame me?"

Thad shook his head. What TJ had said made sense. Still, he didn't feel right about letting Jared go off with a man who was concealing a firearm on his person.

But he never got a chance to discuss or even broach his misgivings with Jared. Thad had never seen anyone work so fast before. After he finished kissing TJ, Jared whispered something in his ear, flicked the lobe with his tongue, and like so many, many men before him, TJ was helpless to do anything other than follow Jared home.

With equal parts jealousy, sadness, joy, and misgivings, Thad watched as they readied themselves to leave the bar. Jared leaned close to him and kissed him as he was getting ready to depart with TJ. "Sorry about leaving you here by yourself."

"It's okay, buddy. It's the law of the jungle. You found a man."

Jared grinned. "Maybe you'll get lucky too. Once word gets around that a prize like you is sitting unescorted at the bar, they will be lining up to vie for your affection."

"You're too kind. I don't know if I'm ready for that yet. Sam..."

Jared put up a hand. "I don't want to hear it. Let yourself have some fun. But just be careful." Jared leaned in even closer to whisper, "There's a full moon outside. If you leave alone, I want you to promise me you'll have 'Sweet Cheeks' call you a cab, okay?"

Thad nodded. It was a good idea. "You be careful. That guy is carrying a gun!"

"I know. And I hope it's a six-shooter!" Jared winked, and before Thad could think of a comeback, he was headed out the door with TJ, who had already placed a protective hand on his ass.

Chapter Fifteen

"Give me a call sometime. We'll do it again." Jared pressed the folded-up Post-it note into TJ's hand. TJ had left Jared feeling worn out and barely able to walk. Later Jared would have to tell Thad about this encounter, make him jealous by letting him in on how he'd found a man with eleven inches. But that was for morning...

"I'll call you again, for sure. What are you doing next Wednesday?" TJ's dark-brown eyes gazed into Jared's blue ones.

Jared cocked his head, exhausted. He could barely think about the next few minutes, let alone next Wednesday, so he just said, "Call me...or send me a text. I'm sure we can set something up." He stood on tiptoe to plant a lingering, deep kiss on TJ. "Meanwhile, I need some time to rest up and recuperate so I can be ready for you again."

TJ laughed. Jared laughed. They made the usual promises to see one another again soon, which both knew they might or might not keep. And then Jared playfully pushed TJ out the door, shut it behind him, and then turned to lean against the door, arms across his chest. It was his first sexual encounter in over a month, some kind of record for him. He didn't think he had gone so long without sex since he was a teenager, a span of a good ten years.

The past month had been hard. Hard for Jared to shake the images of *that night* away from his conscious mind. Even when he succeeded, his subconscious often undermined his efforts, dredging up the gory imagery while he slept, causing him to wake sweating, twisted in his sheets, and with his throat raw from screaming. Once he calmed down, he would wonder what the neighbors thought of the shrieks coming from his apartment in the middle of the night.

Knowing me, they most likely think I was having a good time.

It was also hard for Jared to be out at night alone, to walk the streets of Capitol Hill, which he knew so well and once found so comforting. The recent past had made those same streets fraught with danger, where every footfall behind him was a pursuer, where every shadow hid a hound from hell, and where every unexpected sound—the phone ringing, a floorboard creaking in the hallway outside his apartment, a car backfiring—made him jump and set his heart to pounding.

He didn't even know if he could have crossed the threshold tonight without the inducement of the beer, Thad's company, and the absolutely irresistible denim-sheathed bulge that lay way too long on TJ's left thigh.

Jared was glad, as he locked the deadbolt and the chain lock and headed into his bedroom, that he had made some progress. *And that I've finally gotten laid!* His butt felt tender and sore, but in a good way. He couldn't wait to call Thad in the morning and tell him all about it.

*

He raises his snout to sniff the air and to take in the glorious sight of the full moon, looking pewter against a sky of almost black. Stars twinkle, and the air has a cold snap to it that he loves. The wind rustles his fur. In the air the scent of sex and filth drifts by as a man makes his way down the sidewalk, his shoulders hunched against the cold wind.

In the shadows he watches the man, knowing from where he has come. Other than the human's movement down the hill, things are quiet at this late night hour. The beast can actually move along the sidewalk without being noticed.

But it's the alley behind the small redbrick apartment building to which he is drawn. He looks up and sees a light in one of the rooms go off. He moves around to the back of the building, with its wooden staircases and landings, and looks up to see another light turn on.

He takes the steps quickly, moving toward the light.

*

Jared switched on his bedroom light and grinned as he surveyed the mess. The comforter lay in a wad on the floor, and the sheets hung half off the bed, the striped mattress ticking showing beneath. He was grateful for the glass top covering the cherrywood nightstand next to his bed, because it was sticky with lube and littered with three or four torn condom wrappers.

"Oh, what a night," Jared sang, grinning.

The room smelled of semen and sweat, and Jared paused in the doorway to sniff and consider how long it had been since his room had smelled this way. *Too long.*

On the TV/DVD player combo atop his dresser, a porn still played, the moans and grunts of the men in the sling gangbang scene still going at it, endlessly tireless.

Jared picked up the sticky remote and switched off the power. *Enough of that.* The sex had been great, but tonight Jared knew only too well the meaning of the word *satiated.* Watching more porn right now would be about as exciting as surveying a buffet after consuming a six-course meal.

Jared knew he should change the sheets, take a shower, spritz a little Febreze in the room, but he was just too tired. Slowly, he did manage to stoop and pull the comforter from the floor and fling it over the soiled sheets. He pulled an extra blanket out of his closet. Lying atop the comforter with the blanket over him would be clean enough for tonight. Hell, he was so tired, he could probably drift off in the bathtub if he needed to. He smiled as he dropped his boxers to the floor, turned off his bedside floor lamp, and crawled into bed.

It took him only minutes to fall asleep.

*

The room goes dark as he paces the landing that runs along the back of his prey's apartment. He turns his head to peer in one of the windows. His night vision is good, and he can easily make out the trappings of a kitchen, the appliances, a bowl of apples on the counter, dishes draining beside the sink.

How will he get inside?

If he cocks his head, ears upraised, and really listens, he can hear the sound of his prey snoring...the slow intake and pushing out of breath. If he sniffs near the bottom of the back door, he can even extract the smell of his prey among the other scents and odors trickling out underneath the wooden door. The smell of him is young, clean, and endlessly tantalizing.

He licks his chops.

He raises up on his hind legs to peer into another window, this one farther back and positioned high on the wall. Inside, his victim slumbers, cocooned in blankets and pillows. If he had the muscles for it, he would smile at the scene. It's amusing to him that the young man inside, the young man to whom he plans to do grievous bodily harm as soon as he can figure out a way to get inside, sleeps so soundly and so innocently, unaware that mortal danger lurks only feet away. He backs and attempts to resume his stance on all fours. As he does so, he bumps a potted plant, which topples over, spilling dirt and dried leaves on the wooden surface of the porch.

The plant makes a dull thud. He whimpers softly to himself, hoping no one has heard.

*

Jared awakened with a start, flung from a deep, dreamless sleep with no transition into wakefulness, the landing harsh. Turning onto his back, he listened, alert for any unusual sound. He wasn't aware of what could have awakened him, but his senses were in overdrive.

There's something out there.

Jared curled into a small ball and pulled the blanket over his head, as he had once done as a child tormented by nightmares or the fear of the darkness inside a closet where the door had been left partially open. It got hot quickly under the blanket, but Jared was afraid to emerge. His heart thudded in his chest, blood pounded in his temples, and his stomach twisted with nauseous terror.

He had been waiting for this night. Something irrational and purely instinctual told him that the creature he had seen kill his one-night stand a month ago had now found him and was back to reclaim him, to make sure no witnesses existed. The thought sent an icy glissando of fear up and down his spine.

What was that? It sounded like a whimper.

Jared tried to tell himself he was imagining things. With all the resolve he had, he attempted to calm his racing thoughts by telling himself that any sounds he heard could easily be attributed to the wind outside, or the movements of a neighbor, or even yet another late-night Seattle drizzle just beginning.

But he knew the beast, with its black eyes, its black fur, and—worst of all—its fangs, was just outside, pacing along the landing that ran beside his kitchen and bedroom.

It had found him.

Do I just lie here and wait for it to crash through a window and take me? Do I make myself easy prey? In spite of his thudding heart and the sweat now making his hair wet and stinging his eyes, Jared forced himself to throw off the blanket and slowly sit up.

It was then he noticed his own two dogs, looking strange in the darkness. They both sat at the threshold of his bedroom, bodies alert, ears upraised. Both of them growled low, almost like a hum.

So Jared knew this wasn't his imagination. His dogs heard it too. They were hyperaware. Jared forced himself to swing his legs over the edge of the bed. He trembled but managed to get to a standing position.

The window in his bedroom was a high rectangle near the ceiling. It afforded both light and privacy. But it was too high for Jared to see out of. With a churning in his gut that made him fear he would vomit, he forced himself to climb atop the dresser, where he knelt and peeked just above the windowsill. He feared one look outside would reveal a yellow-eyed, fanged beast from hell staring back at him.

It took a moment or two for Jared's eyes to adjust to the darkness outside, but because of the full moon, a coat of silver blanketed the back landing.

And just as he feared, it was out there. He could make out its supine black form, stretched out at his back door. As Jared watched, he noticed the thing's tongue loll out, dripping as it panted.

It was waiting.

Jared remained frozen, kneeling atop the dresser, unsure what to do.

Call the police? And tell them what?

Open the door and sic the dogs on it? And jeopardize their lives? No way.

Stay here, on top of the dresser, and hope the thing doesn't try to get in by breaking down my door or bursting through a window? I don't fancy being a sitting duck.

Jared thought that perhaps the dawn would chase the beast away, but how long away was that? He slowly rotated his head to look behind him, peering at the red numbers of his alarm clock in the darkened room. It was only three fifteen. The dawn—and morning light—was still hours away.

What with his terror and his cramped position atop the dresser, Jared felt his muscles growing stiff and achy. He backed silently off the dresser and lowered himself to the floor. His movement sent his own two dogs to pacing and whimpering. They knew something was just beyond their back door.

Jared stooped to find a pair of jeans and a sweatshirt among the heaps of clothing on the bedroom floor. Somehow being naked made him feel more vulnerable, even as his rational mind informed him that the clothes would offer little to no protection against powerful jaws and razor-sharp fangs. They had done nothing for poor Hector...

With the dogs at his heels, he crept silently to the back door. He didn't know from where he was getting his courage, but he refused to simply allow himself to become a trembling target for this thing.

At the kitchen door, he pulled aside the curtain and looked outside once again. The dogs scratching and whining at the door's wooden surface made the beast leap to its feet.

Jared couldn't help it. He screamed. He backed away from the window, gibbering in terror, the capacity to form words lost to his horrified brain. The dogs went crazy at the door, leaping against it, scratching and barking, whining and howling.

A scent, like sour sweat, garlic, and overripe meat, seeped through the crack between the bottom of the door and the floor.

Worst of all, the thing stared at him through the glass.

Jared had now reached the wall opposite the kitchen door window and flattened himself against it. His crotch was wet and he wanted to scream, but he had no air left in his lungs to summon one. Or maybe the connection between his brain and vocal cords had been severed by the specter of this monster at his back door. Framed in silvery light, the creature truly looked like something that had escaped from hell. Its eyes blazed, and its mouth hung partially open in a whining snarl that revealed its yellowing—and lethal—fangs. It clawed at the glass, making a shrieking noise on the smooth surface.

*

Fear. It is like a drug to him. Watching his prey pinned against the wall, shaking and breathing hard, only ups his desire to be inside, to rip out his throat and taste the flesh and blood. The wide, terrified eyes would make him want to smile, were he in his human form. But he can only pant and stare, knowing his ferocious gaze ratchets up the horror in his victim.

He whines and scratches at the glass. He knows it will be easy to simply break it and leap into the lair of his prey. But it's more exciting—more tantalizing—to watch the young man cower.

This is a moment to be savored.

He wishes he could let out one baleful howl or a vicious growl, but he needs to keep quiet. Once the glass is broken, he will have to feed quickly. The shattering will wake neighbors, who may alert the authorities.

And he must never, ever be captured.

That truth must not be revealed. He has far too much to lose.

But enough... Food waits for him. Hot, terrified food...

*

Jared knew what it felt like to be utterly and completely paralyzed by terror. He couldn't move if he wanted to. His mind was coherent enough to realize that if the beast crashed through his door at this very moment, he could do little more than mutely stand there and let it rip out his throat.

Finally Jared's adrenaline kicked in enough to allow him to move away from the wall. Just in time too, because the monster outside broke his back window at that moment. The glass shattering sounded like an explosion.

Jared ran, dazed, fevered with fear, into the confines of his own tiny living room. The monster struggled in the kitchen, yelping as the broken glass cut its skin and grunting as Jared assumed it tried to wriggle its massive bulk through the small window.

Oh God, what do I do now? Jared eyed the phone. Putting aside considerations that anyone he would call, in whatever capacity, official or otherwise, would think he was insane, there was the simple truth that whoever might get here to save him could ever make it in time.

His dogs, their brave barking and yapping now replaced by their own terror, raced through the living room together. Jared watched them scurry into the bedroom and dive for cover in the closet. Jack, the pit bull mix, actually hooked a paw around the edge of the closet door to close it more. "Cowards," he whimpered, wondering if he should join them.

He heard a *thud* and realized the thing had gotten inside.

It was panting, and the stink of it once again held Jared frozen in place. But not for long. He turned slowly to grope along the wall, sidling against it until he reached his front door. He quickly and silently turned the deadbolt, then curled his hand around the knob and yanked.

The door opened a few inches...and stopped.

The chain! He had chained the door before falling into bed. With shaking hands he reached up to undo it. Then his hands froze on the chain, because at just that moment, the beast came into the living room. It simply stood there, staring at him. It seemed to be grinning. Jared locked gazes with it, thinking it exuded confidence.

It knows it can kill me easily. I am the sitting duck I feared becoming.

He searched the darkness in vain for his dogs, hoping futilely that they might come to his rescue, but they were nowhere in sight. He didn't blame them. What chance would they have against this monstrous wolfen thing? Jared only hoped they would be able to get away from it, or that it would be satisfied with his blood and not want theirs too.

Jared didn't know if he had the precious few seconds it would take to turn, undo the chain, and hurry out the door. Those movements would take more time than the beast would need to cross the room.

Wouldn't they?

He had to try. The chain lock gave him a little trouble, even more when he heard the click of animal claws on hardwood, but he did manage to loosen the chain, thinking all the while this was a game for the thing. Cat and mouse. A no-lose competition between hunter and hunted. The beast was probably enjoying his terror, his quaint human attempts to get the upper hand or at least get away.

His throat dry, he flung himself toward the door, yanked it open, and ran. He felt hot breath at his heels.

But by God, he was outside, in the corridor, and the stairs were just ahead. He dashed for them, feeling the swipe of a hot claw cut through his skin as he ran. Once he reached the stairs, he half fell down them, ending up in a heap at the landing.

He stared up into the eyes of the beast, knowing this would be the last thing he would ever see.

It leaped into the air, fangs bared and growling.

Jared curled into a small ball, praying everything would be over quickly.

He scrunched his eyes together, imagining the impact of the heavy furred body atop his own...and for just one second his mind flashed on something strange: Thad. *Goodbye, my love. So much for missed opportunities.*

But all was cut short as the blast of a gun rang through the air, deafening.

Jared cringed as he felt the scorching heat of the bullet whiz by his ear. The hot smell of cordite filled his nostrils. And then Jared *did* experience the crushing weight of the beast. A dead weight, as the bloody body of the monster crashed down upon him.

Making unintelligible noises, Jared struggled to get out from under the thing, already dripping blood from a clean hole right above its eyes.

Jared curled into a small ball in a corner of the landing, staring, breathless, his heart feeling like it was beating about a thousand pulses per minute. Below him, the door to the lobby opened and closed, but Jared was too late to see who had come to his rescue. All he heard were quickly retreating footsteps.

A scream lodged somewhere within his throat, but right now he was too shocked to let it emerge. He feared the beast, drawing great shuddering breaths before him, might find the energy to arise once more...and finish him off.

Jared watched as the thing died. Watched as he heard the sounds of people moving above him, witnesses, neighbors who had seen it all. They were curiously silent as they moved about. Jared supposed they were as shocked as he.

He looked up at the faces peering down at him from the landing above. It suddenly seemed as though he recognized none of them, although he had lived in this same building for the past four years. His ears rang. He didn't know if it was from the gunshot moments ago, or if there was something seriously wrong with him.

The faces above him swam in and out of darkness. Jared tried to swallow and found no moisture in his mouth. He tried to part his lips to say something to the by turns sympathetic, shocked, and disapproving faces above him, but nothing came out.

The faces went dark once more, and Jared toppled over onto the landing.

When he awakened, a woman he now remembered was named Grace crouched beside him and placed a cool washcloth on his forehead. She was a cherub-faced woman with lots of tattoos and dyed black hair. Near Grace stood several other people. It was as though fainting had rebooted his brain. He recognized the couple, Frank and Steve, who lived next door to him—and with whom he had once had a passionate three-way—and the Asian woman from two doors down who kept to herself.

He licked his dry lips and said to Grace, "What will we do about the wolf?"

Grace cocked her head, and her face filled with concern. A strand of black hair dropped down over her eyes. She wore a quilted bathrobe, and Jared remembered, oddly, that his mother used to have one like it.

"What are you talking about, honey?"

"The wolf. The monster." Jared licked his lips again and felt silly saying it, but said it anyway. "You know, the *werewolf.*"

"Hush now. There's no such thing."

Jared got up to a sitting position. "Of course there is! It's lying right there..." his voice trailed off as he looked to where the beast had lain at his feet, a bullet hole between its eyes.

But now he saw only the body of a man lying there. Naked. Hairy and packed with hard muscle. The black stubble on his head looked coarse but perfectly complemented the smooth olive of his complexion. His lips were full, his nose Roman, and his face shadowed by a heavy beard. He would have been hot, had it not been for the bullet hole in his forehead.

Had it not been for the fact he was dead...

Chapter Sixteen

Thad hadn't slept when he got home from his outing with Jared. He'd followed his friend's advice when he left the bar, having "Sweet Cheeks" call a cab for him. Once he got home, he stood outside, watching the yellow taxi as it faded off into the distance and the darkness, and looked up at the full moon, which seemed distant, although its silvery light still managed to lend a black-and-white illumination to his familiar neighborhood.

Thad had hoped that all the alcohol he had imbibed would help him fall into a quick, deep, and dreamless slumber, akin to passing out. But the ride home and now the cold night air seemed to have the opposite effect. He was wide-awake, nerves tingling.

And wondering about Sam.

He shook his head, knowing he shouldn't do it, but he stood on the sidewalk and pulled his cell phone from his pocket. He remained drunk enough to leave inhibitions about the late night—or early morning—hour on a shelf and punched in Sam's cell number.

Voice mail.

He punched in the landline for the apartment.

Answering machine.

He dialed the Blue Moon Café.

"Thank you for calling the Blue Moon Café, where old world Italy meets Seattle and the result is *delicioso*. We are currently closed, but if you'd like to make a reservation—" Thad pressed the button to stop the call.

He told me he wouldn't be home. He told me he had to go out of town. Yeah, and where have I heard that song and dance before? Why, surprise, surprise… from Sam!

Thad wondered what was really going on.

And as thousands of drunken, spurned lovers have done since the dawn of time, he turned his thoughts to suspicion and, more specifically, suspicion that there was someone else in the picture.

Thad considered briefly going inside and getting Edith, taking her out for a walk. It would be the sensible thing to do and perhaps give him time to calm the irrational thoughts going through his head. But another voice answered that Edith was most likely fast asleep and would continue to be so until morning. Edith could wait.

So what was stopping him from doing what good sense and propriety told him not to? *Nothing at all*, Thad told himself as he began to walk rapidly toward the lake and the Blue Moon Café.

I am going to get to the bottom of this. Tonight.

As he walked, he thought of Jared and his black stud, pictured them naked and in all sorts of different positions. The thought excited him until the images morphed into Sam with another guy, who stayed faceless in Thad's imaginings, although he had a better, more ripped body than Thad did, and a bigger dick.

Stop it! Thad forced the offending images to scurry from his conscious mind. He considered going home and just getting into bed. He knew tomorrow he would pay in more ways than one for all the martinis and the lack of sleep, not to mention barging in on Sam like an irrational and enraged jealous lover.

Which is what I am.

Thad picked up his pace, and before he knew it, he stood in front of the Blue Moon Café, sizing up the place like a burglar, his breath coming out in puffs of steam floating on the cold night air.

What the hell am I thinking of doing? Am I going to slip around back to peep in the windows? Maybe I'll succeed in scaring Sam's poor mother out of her wits. Maybe Graziela will be waiting for me with a shotgun, a baseball bat, or a knife. She seems like a fighter, that one. Or maybe I'll look into Sam's bedroom and see what his secret is...and if it is, indeed, another man. Or maybe I'll see him in bed with his brother, Giovanni, and uncover the shameful family secret.

This last thought made Thad laugh out loud. He caught himself and looked around empty Green Lake Way to see if anyone had heard him.

I'm turning into a lunatic. Go home. Go home.

Thad shook his head, pulled out his cell, and tried Sam's numbers once more. And once more got the same result.

Why should anyone answer, stupid? They're probably all asleep!

Thad was on his way behind the building to do the Peeping Tom routine he had warned himself about when his cell phone began playing its familiar ringtone. *Thank God, it's Sam. He's calling me back.* The alcohol and his wounded heart conspired to create immediately a scene where Sam beckoned Thad inside and they would have a passionate reunion on a chopping block in the kitchen.

But when he glanced down at the display of his phone, he was disappointed to see it was only Jared calling him. *Probably just wants to brag about the fucking he got at the hands of that thug, TJ. I don't know if I wanna hear it...* Thad pressed the Accept button anyway.

"What? Did you have a hot time?" Suddenly weariness washed over Thad. It caught up with him all at once, making him feel like a fool out there alone in the middle of the night, planning to spy on a lover who most likely wasn't even home.

Jared didn't say anything for several moments. But Thad could hear his breath, which sounded shaky and rapid, panting almost.

"Look, sweetheart, I'm really not in the mood for an obscene phone call. And if you're calling me while engaged in some filthy act of sexual congress, well, I am so not in the mood."

"Thad?"

All at once Thad's mood shifted to red alert. He could sense the terror in his friend's voice in the plaintive way he spoke his name. He mashed the little cell closer to his ear. "Jared? Are you okay?" *I knew that guy TJ was trouble!*

Jared's voice came out in a quivering sigh.

"Jared? Honey, what happened?" Thad found his worries and heartache about Sam replaced by concern over Jared. He couldn't bear it if his friend was hurt... He knew he should have stopped him from going home with TJ. "Is it TJ? Did he hurt you?"

Jared's voice was small. "No. No, nothing like that. Can you come over? Right now? I need you."

Thad was about to tell him he was on his way, but Jared had already hung up.

He ended the call and looked up at the sky, which had turned to dull pewter gray. Dawn was arriving, and it had chased away the full moon. He looked over at the café and a light came on inside, in the back, in the kitchen. He was torn for only a few moments.

Jared needed him. He placed another call on his cell, this time to the cab company.

Chapter Seventeen

The cab had to drop Thad off down the block from Jared's apartment building. When he stepped out of the taxi, Thad felt like he was stepping into a movie set. The front of Jared's building blazed with light from TV crews and the flashing illumination from the roofs of Seattle police vehicles. Two-way radios squawked, audible even from where Thad stood in awe. He spied the familiar yellow of crime scene tape outside the building and draped over wooden horses. A crowd had gathered at the curb, watching the scene. Thad moved closer.

"Hey, man, do you know what happened? Somebody said something about a murder down there." An older guy, midfifties, stopped Thad as he headed toward the flashing lights and noise.

A sick wave washed over Thad. "Was it another of those same killings?"

"What do you mean?" The older man eyed him through rimless glasses.

"You know," Thad said impatiently. "The gay killings."

"You mean the werewolf?"

Thad looked toward Jared's building. He was only a few paces away. *Oh God, please don't let this involve Jared. I don't think I could bear it.* Thad closed his eyes for a minute and drew in a deep breath in a futile effort to calm his jangling nerves and thundering heart.

"I don't think so. What I heard was a shooting."

Thank God.

What am I thinking! Thank God? For a shooting? What's wrong with me? At least it wasn't another of the killings where some poor guy was ripped to shreds. Maybe this was a robbery gone bad, something mundane like a drug- or gang-related murder.

Thad never thought he would look at such horrible crimes and loss of life as a relief. Yet he did. At least it gave him a small measure of hope for Jared's safety.

He looked toward the street to see that the crowd had parted. Slack-jawed, he watched as paramedics wheeled a stretcher out of Jared's front door. Atop it was a black rubber body bag, its zipper closed. For a moment it seemed all went hushed on the street. Thad looked to the older man he stood beside, who had also gone silent as he watched the grisly procession. He tapped the guy. "I gotta go."

Thad started walking briskly toward Jared's building. Just because it was a shooting—*and who knows if the guy on the street was even right about that?*—didn't mean Jared wasn't involved.

It doesn't mean it's not Jared in that bag.

Violence happens all the time, most of it not perpetrated by werewolves.

Thad had a queasy feeling in his gut, a terror he couldn't deny as he hurried to the front of the apartment house where his friend lived.

TJ had had a gun. I knew I shouldn't have let Jared go home with him!

As he neared the house, he stopped at the cordoned-off yard and struggled to make his way through the surging crowd. As he shouldered his way through to the front, a uniformed police officer put a hand on his chest. "I need you to stay behind the line, sir."

"But my friend lives in there! He could be that guy on the stretcher!" Thad cried.

"I'm sorry, sir. This is a crime scene. We can't allow you any farther."

"But can you at least tell me who the victim was? Please, officer, I'm begging you."

The cop shook his head. "Body hasn't been identified yet. Sorry." He walked away.

Helplessly, Thad watched as the paramedics loaded the stretcher into an ambulance.

And then he saw something that lightened his heart, that almost made him laugh out loud with glee and relief.

Jared.

Blinking at the lights, reporters, and cops all gathered outside, he emerged from the building looking shaken and numb. His mouth hung open, and his eyes had a glazed aspect to them. He had a blanket thrown over his shoulders, and his feet were bare.

Isn't he cold? Thad wanted to take off his own shoes to give to Jared.

He looked so hurt and vulnerable, it was all Thad could do not to push the officers standing guard out of his way so he could run to Jared and take him in his arms.

What happened?

Finally, Thad could stand the suspense and the helplessness no longer. Eye contact and telepathy directed toward his friend were not working, so Thad called, "Jared! Jared! It's me."

Jared slowly turned his head, and it took him several minutes scanning the faces of the crowd until his gaze lit on Thad. He stared at him for a bit, until Thad wasn't sure if his friend even recognized him, then gave him a cockeyed grin. Jared trotted over to Thad, a uniformed police officer close behind. Jared said over his shoulder, "This is my friend. I need to talk to him."

"What happened, Jared? What happened? Are you okay?"

Jared shrugged. "I guess. I almost died tonight."

Shock rattled through Thad; he took a step back. "Was it that guy TJ? Was he involved?"

"I suspect he was involved, but he's long gone. And no, he didn't hurt me. He saved me, I think."

"I don't understand."

"I don't either." Jared scratched his head. "Listen, I need to get some different clothes on and then go down to police headquarters and give a formal statement. After that I'll come to you, okay? I'm sorry I made you come out like this, but when I called you, I didn't know what else to do. I'll tell you the whole story then. Can you wait?"

"I don't know. Who was on the stretcher?"

Jared took on a faraway look. He shivered. "We can talk about that later. Okay? I don't know if I'm ready to process this yet. Maybe getting it all out downtown will let me tell you what happened. You will *so* not believe it."

Thad watched, confused, as Jared walked away with the officer.

*

When Thad returned home, tendrils of warm, burnished light crept over the eastern horizon. His apartment building looked golden in the soft-focus illumination. Thad wished his own mood matched the tranquility of the early morning. He hurried inside, where Edith waited by the door. If he could anthropomorphize her, he would have had her with her forepaws crossed over her chest, asking in a sullen voice, "Where have you been?"

"Come on. Come on. I know you have to do your business. I know you're hungry." Thad stooped to affix leash and harness to the dog, grabbed a tiny Nine West dog sweater at the last minute, and put that on her too. It was cold. Heading out the door, he pondered how grounding it was to have a dog in his life. As he watched Edith sniff a bush, then squat to pee beside it, he thought no matter what was going on—love affairs, shootings, werewolf murders—Edith stayed true to her agenda of short walks with bathroom breaks, two square meals a day, and lots of sleep.

He loved the dog simply because she was so uncomplicated. Unlike everything else in his life...

They hurried back inside Thad's studio. He opened the blinds a little to let in the early morning light. The day looked like it was shaping up to be a sunny one, but Seattle was full of false promises when it came to sunny mornings. The days often ended up with gray clouds, rain, and wind.

Thad sat down on the bed, feeling numb and sore. A headache buzzed just behind his eyes. He knew he needed desperately to sleep. Going all night without some of that magic REM stuff was not good for one's health or one's psyche.

Yet he knew even if he lay back on the bed, as his weary body urged him to do, his racing mind—so full of questions—would not let him drift off. He thought of that old Robert Frost poem and the line in it that went something like "and miles to go before I sleep." He reflected that the same poem also spoke of woods that were "lovely, dark, and deep," and the thought gave him an odd chill. He called Edith to him, and when the dog hopped up on the bed, Thad pulled her onto his lap.

What had happened to Jared?

Where was Sam?

Were the two things related?

Thad shook his head. He didn't want to ponder how, during the past two full moons, Sam and his family were not around. He didn't want to think that during both of those nights, someone was killed.

He also didn't want to remember—oh God, he really did not want to recall *this*—that he had told Sam about his "date" with Jared yesterday, told him, in fact, what Jared's last name was and the street where he lived.

Why did I do that?

To make Sam jealous.

And what if I did make him jealous? What would Sam do?

Thad felt sick as he pictured the black body bag being removed from Jared's building.

Was Sam inside the bag?

Was Sam the werewolf killer?

He pictured Sam in his mind's eye, naked. The man was covered in black hair, his beard thick, his eyes dark and, yes, almost feral. One could easily say he was wolfen. Thad remembered how Sam would bite him when he made love to him, how their sex could sometimes be almost brutal, like animals. He had loved Sam's hairiness and adored the rough sex they shared. Both were hot. Exciting.

But were both deadly?

He couldn't believe Sam was a killer. After the rough sex, Sam had always been incredibly tender, touching him gently, covering him with small kisses, and singing to him in Italian. And other times he was so concerned that Thad was well fed. Sam was a nurturer. Kindness radiated off him. He couldn't kill anyone... Could he?

But what if something happened to him during the full moon, something beyond his control? What if Sam simply could not help himself? The werewolves in movies were sometimes remorseful for what they had done when they morphed into their bestial selves. Perhaps the same was true of Sam.

Thad couldn't stand just sitting here on his bed. The questions would torment him until he drove himself insane. He stood, shrugged into a fleece and his Kangol knit cap, and headed out the door.

The Blue Moon Café was only a couple of blocks away. As Thad approached the restaurant, he grew apprehensive. The place was ablaze with lights. Sam had told him they would talk once the time was right. Thad could think of no time more right than the present. Even though a part of him trembled with fear and uncertainty, he forced himself to march right up to the plate glass front door of the café.

He stopped when he saw the sign, hand-lettered, that had been affixed to the door.

Closed Due to Death in the Family

Thad stepped back, reeling. This was all too much.

It was Sam! It was! Everything I worried about is true!

Thad shook his head and tried to reassure himself that he knew nothing, not with even the smallest degree of certainty. It could have been their old mother who had passed away...or even more likely, the grandmother.

Thad couldn't help himself. He began banging on the plate glass, praying silently to see Sam emerge from the back.

But he didn't get his wish. Graziela stormed toward the front of the restaurant, her hair wild, swinging behind her, her eyes ablaze with rage. Even at this early morning hour, she wore a form-fitting black dress, high heels, and her lips were a scarlet slash. She didn't look pleased to see Thad.

She struggled for a moment with the lock and then flung open the door, glaring at him. Before Thad could say even one word, she started in on him, "Didn't you see the sign? We are in mourning, you silly boy. Take your puppy dog eyes and your queer face away from here...right now."

Thad was stunned by her words. "Was it Sam? Please tell me it wasn't Sam..." He felt tears prick the corners of his eyes. He knew it was Sam.

Graziela's lips seemed to disappear into a thin horizontal line of fury. "We have a tragedy here. And places to go and things to do more important than your silliness. Go away!"

She slammed the door, locked it, and walked away from him. She paused at the other side of the room to switch off the lights in the café.

Thad stared at the sign again.

Closed Due to Death in the Family

Thad hunched his shoulders against the wind and walked away from the restaurant, his head hung low. If it *was* Sam, he supposed he would find out soon enough.

*

As he neared his apartment, he heard the ringtone of his cell coming from his pocket. Would he never sleep? He pulled the phone out and glanced down at the Caller ID. It was Jared.

He pressed Talk. "Are you okay? Are you home?"

"I'm in a cab and almost to your place. I needed to talk to you face-to-face. Here I am now."

And Thad turned to see the yellow cab making its way down his street. He stood watching—gratefully—as Jared exited the cab. They must have given him time to dress, because gone was the blanket ensemble he had seen him in earlier. Jared wore a pair of jeans, a hooded University of Washington sweatshirt, and a white fleece jacket. His blond hair looked clean, catching the morning light. He seemed, at least at this moment, no worse off for what had happened to him.

Thad smiled as Jared approached him. Thad pulled Jared close, hugging him tightly, almost as if he wanted to squeeze all the trauma Jared had been through recently right out of him. He held Jared close for several minutes, not thinking about anything beyond this moment and not caring either what the neighbors must be thinking. At last he held Jared out from him at arm's length and regarded him. "You're really okay? Tell me you're okay. That's all that really matters."

"I'm okay, Thad. Really. Can we go in? It's cold out here."

"And you need to tell me everything." Thad led him inside.

Once Thad had put on the coffee and some comforting Joshua Bell on the violin in the background, he sat down with Jared.

"So?"

Jared settled back into the couch and closed his eyes. He took a few breaths, deep, even ones, before beginning. "It's over. I'm safe. The monster is dead."

The words sent an icy shiver through Thad. He could not help but wonder if he was intimately acquainted with the "monster." The handwritten sign on the door of The Blue Moon Café flashed in his mind: Closed Due to Death in the Family.

A queasiness, twisting his gut, followed up the icy chill. He tried to be happy for Jared, to rejoice in the fact that he believed he was now out of danger, but the fear that somehow Sam was involved in all this persisted.

"What do you mean? The monster? Do they know who it was?"

Jared opened his eyes and leveled his gaze upon Thad, smiling. "They do. But what's more important is that I do. And I did the minute I saw those eyes from hell looking in my kitchen window at me, like I was the beast's next meal."

Jared told him the whole story about his night with TJ, about waking up later, and the noises and the terror—the dogs growling and alert. About the wolfen creature on his back landing. And the gunshot that felled him.

"That was TJ? I mean, who shot the wolf?"

Jared nodded. "I think so. Whoever did it was out of the building so fast, I didn't get a chance to see. But my neighbor, Grace Wallensky, looked out her window after the shot, and she saw a black man in a leather coat running like hell down the street." Jared swallowed. "I think it was him. I think he might have even seen the wolf as it was heading to my back door and wanted to protect me." All at once Jared's features twisted into pure terror, his eyes sparkling with it, and his lips parted to draw in small panting breaths. "If he hadn't been there, I don't know what would have happened." Jared fell silent. "Well, actually, I do. I would have ended up like those other guys—shredded and partially eaten." A shiver, almost like a seizure, coursed through him. He hugged himself tightly.

Thad threw an arm over his friend's shoulder and pulled him close. "It's over now. You *are* safe, and you're here with me." Thad waited. He let Jared's breathing return to normal before he asked his next question. He *had* to know. "So when they carried the wolf out, was it—"

Jared suddenly sat forward, turning toward his friend. "That's it! That's the thing I haven't told you! They didn't carry out a wolf." Jared paused. "They carried out a man."

Even though he knew, in some weird instinctive way, precisely what he meant, Thad asked anyway. "What do you mean, 'they carried out a man'?" *I don't want to hear it. I don't want to hear it.*

"It was just like in the movies, man. The thing *morphed.* One minute I was looking at this salivating, dying, big old nasty-ass wolflike thing, and the next thing I know, I looked again and there was a naked man lying there on the floor at my feet. With a bullet hole in his head."

"You dreamed this." Thad was not above grasping at straws.

"What? Haven't you listened to a word I've said?"

"Yes. I just don't know if I want to believe it."

Jared regarded him, eyebrows raised. It was obvious this reaction was not what he had expected. "What's with you? I don't get it. I thought you'd be happy for me, happy this whole shitty nightmare was over, and yet you seem— I don't know—suspicious?"

Thad drew in a quivering breath. "It's not like you think, sweetie. I'm not suspicious. I'm worried."

"Huh?"

"What did the man look like? You know, the dead one?" Just saying "dead" when Sam's image floated in his mind made Thad want to puke. He felt torn between elation that his friend had been spared a gruesome and grisly death and the very real fear that a man he thought he loved was in fact a monster. A monster that could kill his best friend...

A monster that's now dead.

"He looked...good. I mean, he was kind of hot. That's weird for me to say, isn't it?"

Thad reared up and stood in front of Jared. *I have to know.* "Did he have a beard? Was he hairy? Muscular? Olive complexion?" He sucked in more air, but it seemed the supply of oxygen in the room was rapidly dwindling. "Did he have a tattoo?"

Thad waited.

Jared scratched his head, and Thad could see him thinking, his brows furrowing in concentration. "Yeah— yeah, he did. How did you know?"

Thad wished he *didn't* know. He bit his lower lip hard as several emotions coursed through him—grief, sadness, terror, horror—all mixed up in a potent brew that made him both want to cry and to laugh hysterically. *I have to know.* "I just do. Tell me what that tattoo looked like."

Or don't. Maybe I don't want to hear the answer. Thad felt like the next words to come out of Jared's mouth were akin to a train hurtling toward him. He was trapped on the tracks and had nowhere to escape to.

"Weird. I really couldn't see it that well, but now that I think about it, it looked like a—"

Thad cut him off. "Like a wolf? Suckling two baby boys?" Thad sat down hard on the couch next to Jared. He leaned forward, covering his face with his hands.

"That's right." Jared's voice was full of wonder. "You knew." Thad felt Jared gently push him back against the couch and then tug Thad's hands away from his face so Jared could look at him. "How did you know that, Thad? Tell me."

Thad couldn't get his brain and tongue to function together. He wanted to answer Jared but couldn't, not right at this moment. He wondered if what he felt was what one experienced when going into shock.

Jared went on, "You couldn't have guessed that." Jared pulled at Thad's face so their eyes met. "You know who this was, don't you?"

Thad nodded. "I'm going to be sick." He got up and rushed into the bathroom, where he knelt before the toilet and vomited. His eyes got bleary; his nose and throat burned. His face slicked over with sweat.

Jared stood behind him. Thad didn't know if he could talk to him, didn't know if he could tell him the man he loved was the man who almost killed him.

Both of them froze as they heard knocking—more like pounding, really—on Thad's front door. Edith raised a chorus of barks at the sound. Jared looked over his shoulder, back at the door. "Expecting company?"

Thad allowed himself a few tentative swallows, making sure he was done retching. He stood on shaky legs, gripping the sink for support. He mumbled in response to Jared, "Fuck if I know. No, no company." He hunched over the sink, splashed cold water on his face, and rinsed out his mouth. When he rose and saw his reflection, he almost gasped. He was ashen. Dark circles underlined his eyes, eyes that were shot through with red. He looked like hell.

Why shouldn't I? The man I thought I loved is dead. He tried to kill my best friend. He probably killed other gay men in Seattle. My dead love was a werewolf. Why shouldn't I look like I've gone through the wringer? I have. For Christ's sake, I have.

The knocking sounded again, this time even more insistent. Edith continued to yap, now leaping at the door, stopping to claw at it.

"Want me to get that?"

"No." Thad did the routine with the water again and ran damp fingers through his hair. He hurried to where the pounding sounded once more. He wondered what fresh hell was this, nudged Edith gently out of the way with his foot, and flung open the door.

Sam stood there.

Chapter Eighteen

His hand was still upraised, poised to knock again, and as Thad looked him over, Sam's beard and heavy brow failed to hide the flurry of emotions crisscrossing and colliding with one another on his handsome features. He rubbed his hand over his face, as though he were just waking up. He smiled.

Thad felt, probably for the first time in his life, like he was going to faint. This wasn't happening. This was a figment of his imagination. This was a ghost. Or no, there actually *was* someone standing at his door, but it was not Sam. Rather it was a detective from the Seattle Police Department, come to tell him he needed to ask him a few questions. This could not be Sam. Sam had been killed in the stairwell of Jared's apartment building.

Hadn't he?

Apparently not, because as much as Thad tried to tell himself this was not his flesh and blood boyfriend standing there before him, the reality of him—his height, his dark eyes, his beard in need of a trim, the muscles testing the endurance of the pressed white shirt he wore, and yes, even the smell of garlic and basil coming off him—was undeniable. Sam was here. He wasn't dead.

Ergo Sam was not the killer.

Thad was not coordinated enough to put tongue, breath, and brain together to say anything. But he was in command of himself enough to step outside the door, grab

Sam, pull him close, and revel in the simple living, breathing *solidity* of him. He grabbed him and clung to him so desperately, he feared squeezing the life out of him. But he didn't care.

Sam was alive!

Totally unexpectedly, Thad began to weep. He allowed his tears to flow onto Sam's chest. Sam quietly stroked Thad's hair and let him cry. Finally he gently pulled back, his arms remaining on Thad's shoulders.

"We need to talk. I think it's time you knew the truth. *All* the truth."

Thad nodded and just then remembered Jared was still there. He turned to look over his shoulder and saw his friend standing just inside the doorway, watching the scene with a blank expression. Thad figured the poor guy had witnessed so much the previous night and this morning that he was in some sort of sensory overload. He also wondered, as he grasped Sam's hand to lead him inside, what to *do* with Jared. His friend had been through a lot, and Thad didn't want to ask him to leave to be alone after so much trauma. But his apartment was a studio. He couldn't ask Jared to wait in the bathroom while he and Sam talked. Yet he knew Sam would most likely want to be alone to have this discussion...

And what would be said?

Thad shivered as he thought of the possibilities. He also thought that all his imaginings were wild. But how would Sam explain the similarities between him and the dead man in Jared's apartment building? How would he explain the tattoo? Surely this was too much of a coincidence.

After Thad introduced Jared and Sam, the three of them stood awkwardly in the studio. Each eyed the other with wariness. Since it was his place, Thad realized it was up to him to make the next move, but he still didn't have a clue as to what he should do or say next.

Fortunately Jared—God bless him—had the presence of mind to speak. "Looks like you guys could use a little alone time. I'm gonna make myself scarce." He peeked out the window. "The sun is actually shining, and I think I could benefit from a walk around that gorgeous lake."

"Are you sure?" Thad tried to pick up something from Jared's eyes, some reassurance that he would be okay.

"I'm a big boy. I'll be okay. You guys talk, whatever. Don't worry. I'll be back." Jared hurried out before Thad had a chance to protest.

At last he was alone with Sam. His excitement and relief at knowing the man had not been killed had begun to dissipate, but he now realized that he really loved Sam. His joy and elation at seeing him alive told him so. "Let's sit down."

They sat side by side on Thad's love seat. Edith glowered at Sam from the corner, her eyes practically bulging. Thad wondered if he should put her in the bathroom and decided not to. She would have to get used to him someday, somehow. That is, if what Sam was about to tell him didn't change everything.

Thad turned to Sam and kissed him, taking in his smell, his firmness, the taste of his mouth, and then forced himself to pull away. He knew it would be too easy to simply lose himself in the physical, to let the kiss lead to more...and more. To never talk. He wasn't really sure he wanted his wish to know the truth to come true. In the back of his mind, Jack Nicholson thundered, "You can't handle the truth!"

Thad wasn't sure he could. But sometimes life took on its own momentum, regardless of whether we were prepared for where it would take us. Thad let himself settle back into the couch and said, "Tell me."

Sam stared forward, facing the window. He didn't say anything for several minutes, but Thad could see him thinking. The effort of it showed on his furrowed eyebrows, his lips pressed into a thin line, and the way he breathed...a little faster. Finally, he turned to Thad. What he said next shocked Thad so much that he again felt a woozy sensation that caused him to fear he would faint.

"My son died this morning. My Domenic is gone."

That was not what Thad had expected to hear.

Sam attempted to keep his features composed, but it took only seconds for that resolve to crumble. He lowered his head, and Thad didn't know when he'd last seen a grown man cry so openly. Sam sobbed. His shoulders shook. His nose ran, and he wiped at it angrily with his hand. He came very close to wailing.

Even though this was not what Thad had anticipated, unpleasant connections were starting to forge in his mind. He had no time for them right now. Right now he needed to comfort Sam, who had lost his only son. He leaned in and wrapped his arms around Sam, pulling his head down onto his shoulder. Sam quickly dampened that shoulder as Thad helplessly patted his back, wondering what he could possibly say that would lessen Sam's grief.

Finally the only words that could come out of Thad's mouth were simple. "I'm so sorry. What happened?"

It took Sam a long time to get himself under control. But when he did, he regarded Thad with red-rimmed eyes. "You wouldn't believe me."

Thad already had a good idea of what might have happened, but he needed to hear the words from Sam's mouth so he could begin processing them. "I don't know about that. Why don't you just tell me?" *Let's just herd the elephant out of the room. Or should that be wolf?*

Thad felt like he was removed from himself as Sam began to speak, as if he were watching their little heart-to-heart from a distance, and wondered again if the sensation was the beginning of going into shock. Again, what Sam said was not what he had anticipated.

"Domenic had a lot of problems. He could never accept my being gay. When I left his mama to be with another man, Domenic was only nine years old. And he never forgave me." Sam shook his head. "I tried to show him that two men could love one another and that being gay was okay...not a choice, but just a way of being. But all Dom could see was that this was the thing that had destroyed his family."

Thad wasn't sure where this was leading or if it would even end up with talk of murder or werewolves. He hoped, somehow, it wouldn't. But instinct and strong intuition told him otherwise. Thad couldn't sit back and wait in suspense for where he hoped this was *not* leading, so he screwed up his courage and asked, "What does this have to do with Domenic dying?"

"He didn't die. He was killed. Murdered. Assassinated." Sam swallowed, staring intently out the window at the sun-drenched day so at odds with the words being exchanged here and now.

Thad nodded. "He was shot?"

"You heard?" Sam turned to regard Thad, then shrugged. "I suppose it's already on the news."

The ugly, gruesome jigsaw pieces fell rapidly into place.

"Someone killed my boy!" Sam cried, and the tears began to flow once more. Thad didn't hug him this time but sat beside Sam, simply watching.

And did "your boy" try to kill my friend? Did "your boy" kill other innocent gay men? Why? Why, Sam? Because they were like you?

A sluice of ice surged through Thad's veins. *Would he have killed me too...eventually?*

The thought took his breath away.

When Sam's tears again slowed to a trickle and his breathing stopped being hiccupping sobs, he continued, "Yes, they shot my Domenic. Right there on Capitol Hill. I can't blame them. He was trying to kill someone...again." Sam stared at Thad, his eyes pleading, Thad thought, for understanding.

And Thad didn't know if he understood...or if he ever could. He said nothing, which he guessed encouraged Sam to continue.

"He killed another gay man. He has been doing it since we came here."

"You knew it?" Thad's words came out dead, expressionless.

Sam shook his head. "Maybe. Maybe I knew and just didn't want to believe. Fathers can deny a lot about their children. You'd understand if you had a child."

Thad looked over at Edith, who had at last lain down in her bed. She continued, though, to stare at Sam. "I'm not sure I could." Then another thought came to Thad, and it ignited an ember of fury in him. Had Sam lied to him *again*?

"Wait a minute. You told me—a while back—that Domenic had gone home to Italy. I'm sure you told me you sent him back." Thad found he had no spit in his mouth; he couldn't swallow.

"I thought he had. All this time I thought my boy was in Sicily, and he was right here."

"So what happened?"

"Graziela happened."

"What?"

"Graziela has always loved Domenic like her own son. She spoiled him. She doted on him. She probably knew it was him who was killing those men. She didn't care. Like Domenic, she probably thought they got what they deserved." Sam sat forward, hands on knees, so he wasn't looking at Thad. "I trusted Graziela to take him to the airport, to put him on the plane I had bought a ticket for. I even drove them out to SeaTac, and both of us—my sister and me—we saw Domenic through the gates at the international terminal. When I looked up in the sky later, I imagined my boy on that big plane, away from me. I was hoping going home to be with others in our family might help him learn how to behave."

"Behave?" It sounded like Sam was talking about getting a teenage kid to step in line, show some respect for his elders, quit staying out late, drinking and smoking.

"Yes. But he was not on that plane." Sam turned back to Thad, again with the pleading expression in his eyes. "He just stayed in the airport. Graziela went back later and got him, and she's been hiding him from me ever since. They had it all planned." Sam wept softly. "And look what happens."

Thad didn't know what to think, let alone say. He felt numb inside, emotions tamped down to cold embers. He knew that—lurking just behind the numbness—was hysteria, giddy, uncomfortable laughter, and a torrent of tears. But right now all he felt was dead. He suddenly wished he could just stand up and walk out of the studio, slam the door behind him, and never look back. He wanted to erase the fact that he had ever met Sam, that he had ever set foot in the Blue Moon Café, and that he was now ensnared in this whole mess, weird and horrific beyond even his wildest imagining. Most of all he wished he could restore *life* to his gay brethren. No matter what their faults, none of them had deserved the grisly and terrifying ends they'd met. He stared resolutely forward, not trusting himself to even look at Sam. He didn't know what he feared more: that looking at him would incite feelings of love and compassion or, worse, hatred and repulsion. He asked the next question that needed to be asked.

"I feel silly even saying this. Like I'm in a dream, but what about the whole werewolf thing? Is it true? How does that work?"

"Would you look at me? Please." Sam asked plaintively. Thad finally gave in and met Sam's dark-eyed gaze. Thad realized Sam, at this moment, was most likely more afraid of Thad than Thad was of him. He felt a rush of love for the man, in spite of his intellect and common sense telling him not to.

Sam said, "Of course it's true. You know that. There are many things in this world we choose not to acknowledge. Many things hidden in the shadows. Werewolves, as you call them, are one of them."

"So how did Domenic become one?" Thad thought of the movie *An American Werewolf in London* and remembered how the two guys were attacked on the moors. "Did he get bit?"

Sam sucked in a great quivering breath. "No. It doesn't work that way." He stopped.

Thad resisted the suspicions flooding through him, but he had to know. "How does it work, then?"

"Domenic was born a werewolf." Sam caught Thad's hands in his own and held them tight. "His papa is a werewolf, just like his papa before him...and so on."

Thad snatched his hands away. He felt his face go hot and a sudden urge to burst into tears. "You're one too?"

Sam nodded. "And Graziela. And Mama. And Nana. And Giovanni. All the Lupinos. *Lupe* in Italian means wolf."

Thad thought if he had anything left in his stomach, it would have come up. Instead he only felt a sickening acidic taste at the back of his throat. "So... So... Domenic is not the only killer in the family? You kill too?"

Sam tried to reach out to pull Thad close, but Thad shrank away. Sam sadly dropped his arms. "No! No! You don't understand. Just like people have evolved, so have my kind. We do kill, yes, but only animals. I have never— I swear to you—taken another human life. The biggest thing I have ever killed is a deer."

"So, when you disappear? When the moon is full?" Thad feared he was losing the power of coherent speech.

"We hunt. We go to the woods. That's what we loved about Seattle. We can get away into wilderness and mountains so quickly and easily. We kill for food. That's all." Sam stood and crossed to the kitchen area. He opened Thad's freezer and rooted around. "I see you have steak in here, pork chops, chicken." He turned to look at Thad. "You eat dead animals too."

Thad considered becoming a vegetarian. "Yeah, but I don't kill those animals. I don't drink their blood."

"Look. We are different. I don't expect you to understand me all at once. I don't expect you to accept me in one second. But I ask you to try to keep an open mind, to try to understand we hunt for food when the moon is full. We change. I am not the same creature standing before you right now. But I do want you to understand that we are not murderers."

Sam sat back down next to Thad but didn't attempt to take him in his arms. "Something was wrong with my Domenic." He shook his head. "Even if we were not weres, he would maybe have killed, just in a different way." Sam bit his lip, and Thad could tell he was holding back another onrush of tears. Killer or no killer, one's son was one's son, and Thad could only begin to imagine the depths of Sam's grief. Losing a son was horrible enough, but then to realize that son had done awful, evil, and destructive things, Thad was sure was probably almost too much to bear.

He relented and put his arms around Sam.

"You forgive me, then? We can work through this."

Thad pressed his face into Sam's neck, then raised it a little to whisper in his ear. "You're moving too fast. I don't know anything yet. I need time to think. Time to process. And you need time to mourn and bury your son."

Sam clutched at him tightly. "I can't bear not seeing you. I can't bear going through this without you. I need you."

What Sam was saying was perfectly reasonable. Thad just didn't know if reason was enough to overcome the potent brew of emotions—betrayal, horror, and unease chief among them.

He leaned back, taking Sam's bearded face in his hands, and kissed him. Deeply. "Give me one night. Go to your family. Give me today and tonight. We'll talk tomorrow."

Before Sam could respond, they both looked up as the door opened. Edith let out a chorus of barks.

Jared stood in the doorway, framed in golden light.

Sam looked over at Thad. "Okay. Tomorrow, then." He leaned in and kissed Thad.

And then he was gone.

Chapter Nineteen

The next day Thad stood outside the Blue Moon Café, unsure if he wanted to go inside. How far he had come since that first night, that first magical night when Sam fed him in so many ways, when the spark of their love had ignited and burst into flame.

And now look at him. Standing here outside the café in the rain, uncertain of how things would go when he stepped inside. Would he be dissuaded from his common-sense decision by Frank Sinatra or Rosemary Clooney singing about love? By the warm smells of comforting Sicilian food wafting out from the kitchen? And last, and certainly not least, by Sam's formidable presence? He was the most gorgeous and masculine man Thad had ever been with. His physical presence alone pushed all sorts of erotic buttons. But it was not only that. Decency and compassion radiated from the man like body heat.

He stepped up to the front door. Because it was late afternoon, the place was virtually empty. A red-haired woman sat by a rain-smeared window, looking out at the lake across the way, nursing a small cup of espresso. An older man sat hunched over the bar with a glass of beer in front of him. Other than that, the place appeared deserted.

Sam appeared from the back. He wore a white chef's shirt, black-and-white checked pants, and a wary smile.

How can I do this to him when he's just lost his son?

Thad stepped farther inside and returned the smile, although his was small, his lips barely upturned at the corners. He felt a rush of love for Sam and hoped he wasn't confusing it with sympathy or even lust. After all, losing one's child, Thad had heard, was one of the greatest griefs one could experience. And even though Domenic had been an evil killer and probably ruthless and psychotic to boot, as far as Thad knew, he'd still been Sam's only offspring.

Offspring that would have killed my best friend if it had not been for wild coincidence and nearly divine intervention...

Thad moved across the restaurant and, with no urging from Sam, sat down at one of the tables near the back, far away from the man at the bar and the woman at the table near the window. Sam quickly joined him. He took up Thad's hands in his own and leveled his intense stare at Thad. The heat from his hands was electric. Neither of these things made what Thad had come to say any easier.

"Where is everyone? Graziela? Giovanni?" Thad scanned the room for other Lupinos and came up empty.

"They have gone to make arrangements for my boy. We are sending him back to Sicily for the funeral and burial." Sam dipped his head, and Thad could see he was trying mightily not to cry.

I can't do this. I just can't.

I must. Is this the life I want for myself?

Thad nodded. "I'm so sorry about him. Will you go to Sicily too?"

"Of course."

And Sam's simple reply made things easier for Thad. He had come here to end things with him, to tell him the whole werewolf family thing—it all sounded surreal even as he thought the words!—was just too much. He didn't believe he could align himself with such strangeness, no matter how much he loved the man. But maybe Sam being gone for a few days or weeks might grant a little reprieve to the situation. Perhaps this leave of absence could allow Thad to simply postpone, rather than act on, the decision he had made during yet another nearly sleepless night.

The two sat silently for a while. Finally, Sam asked, "So you have thought about things?"

Thad nodded. "I have, and Sam, I want you to know I love you. But I just don't know where we go from here. All of this has been so much, so very much to handle. And I have no experience with such things. Hell, I don't even know if I can believe any of it. I keep thinking this is a dream I will wake up from."

"So you want to break up with me?" Sam's expression was so sad, so plaintive, that it just about broke Thad's heart. He absolutely could not answer in the affirmative to that question. At least not now. What kind of heartless cad would break up with a father who had just lost his only son?

A killer. Don't forget: a killer.

Thad shook his head. "Sweetheart, I honestly don't know what I want. I came here to say goodbye. But now that I sit here, across from your sweet, sweet face, I know I don't have the nerve, or the courage, to do that. Common sense tells me the right thing, the best thing, the only thing to do is to run, not walk, away from you. But my heart tells me differently."

"I'm glad to hear that. Sicilians understand the heart winning out over the head. We make almost all our decisions that way." Sam smiled; then his features darkened. "It's what allowed me to believe, for so long, that my Domenic was just confused and not bad."

"I know."

"So where does this leave us? I was going to ask you to come to Sicily with me. I could use your support."

This last stunned Thad. He would never have expected Sam to ask such a thing. Even though their relationship had progressed over the past few months, he didn't really see himself fitting so intimately into the family. "I can't. I wish I could. And you know you have my support and caring." Thad couldn't take this anymore. He stood up suddenly, almost sending his chair toppling over to the floor.

"I still need time. A month? Who knows? But I will use the time to consider what I can and cannot have in my life, and either way, my love, I will not forget you." Thad wanted to laugh at himself. Even though he was sincere, his words sounded—even to him—like something out of a bad romance novel. He wished he could reel them back in. But he knew, in the end, they were true, and he supposed that was all that mattered.

Sam stared down at the table, then looked up at Thad, his eyes glistening. "That sounds an awful lot like goodbye."

"It's not. I don't know what it is. Take good care of yourself. Take care saying goodbye to your son. You can probably use this time alone yourself."

Sam nodded sadly, saying nothing. "I will be back in a week, ten days at the most. Maybe you will come by the restaurant then? Maybe we'll talk again?" There was a plaintive note in Sam's tone that made Thad ache inside.

Hadn't Sam heard what he had just said about needing at least a month? This was getting out of control.

Thad didn't know how to deal with this situation, and even though part of him told himself to stay, to talk things through, the urge to simply flee was stronger. Part of him wanted to just be young again, unfettered, concerned about things like which bars to go to on the weekend, what online hookup service to use, and what playlist to create next on his iPod. This whole episode in his life had aged him immeasurably. He wondered if he could ever get back to the place he was in before he first walked into the Blue Moon Café and laid eyes on Sam.

"I'm sorry. I have to go. Give my condolences to your family." Thad turned to start walking rapidly from the restaurant. He didn't want Sam to see him cry. But at the door, without caring who heard, he caught Sam's gaze in his own and mouthed the words, "I love you."

Sam smiled. "*Ti adoro,*" he said, so soft Thad barely heard him.

Thad turned and hurried off into the rain.

*

"It's been long enough."

Thad sat in his studio, in front of the TV. *Project Runway* was playing without sound. Thad had muted the TV when the phone rang. Pizza boxes littered the coffee table, along with several empty beer bottles. Clothes made unsightly lumps upon the crumb-infested carpet. Dishes piled high in the sink. Thad listened to Jared breathing through the receiver, waiting. "Long enough for what?"

"Long enough for your period of mourning, for your retreat from society, for you holing up to lick your wounds. Your best friend says it's time for someone else to lick you, or you them. It will do wonders for your state of mind and your spirit. Listen to Mama. She knows."

Thad allowed himself a polite laugh. "What did you have in mind?" Jared had called almost every day or night, sometimes both, for the past two weeks, exhorting Thad to come out with him. He already knew what Jared had in mind. And Thad knew in his heart his best friend was right. It was just easier to put off until another day getting out among people again. It was the same way he procrastinated about searching for a job, cooking something nutritious to eat...showering.

"You know what I have in mind—an evening of revelry. A night of oblivion. Cocktails and cock. Put your troubles behind you. Put a *hot man* behind you. I know it sounds like it's impossible to do, but once you're out there with me, who will ensure that you are having the time of your life, you'll forget about your troubles...at least for one night. And the next night you try will get easier. I promise."

Thad sighed.

"Honey, I care about you. You want me to come over there and help you get ready?"

Thad looked around the mess of his apartment—the filth and the chaos—and knew he'd be ashamed for anyone else to see it. "No."

"You'll come out tonight? We'll meet at ten at the Barça Lounge, okay? I'm buying the first round. And I will defer to you any man in the bar who catches your eye."

"I don't know." Thad took a nibble on a piece of ice-cold, crusty pizza and then a sip of flat, tepid beer. Why was he punishing himself this way?

"Come on..." Jared urged. "Listen, if you get out and find it isn't working, you can go home. It's that simple. I'll even pay for the cab. What have you got to lose?"

Thad looked once more around his sad apartment, currently a shrine to despair and depression, and said, "Nothing. Nothing at all."

"See you at ten?"

"At ten." Thad hung up.

Thad looked at the clock. He had about three and a half hours. If he was going to clean up, he thought it might be easier to begin with his home. He went into the kitchen area, pulled a Hefty trash bag from under the sink, and began loading it up with pizza boxes, beer bottles, and even a few pans that looked beyond scrubbing. He wiped off all the surfaces with either Pledge or Windex and then stuffed a mountain of soiled paper towels into the trash bag. He vacuumed. Started the dishwasher. He shut the TV off and replaced it with the new Adam Lambert CD. He took Edith out for a brisk walk around the block.

Finally he turned to himself. His cleaner surroundings actually did lighten his spirits a bit, making him feel less encumbered by the weight of Sam and the loss of what he had once believed so promising.

He went into the bathroom and laid out one of his only remaining clean towels. He turned the water to hot and adjusted the pressure to jackhammer. He had two weeks of crud to clean off himself. Underneath the shower he began to feel something. And no, not *that* something, but a lifting of his mood, as though simply taking out the trash and ridding himself of the physical evidence of his two black weeks of melancholy had actually removed a physical weight from his shoulders. He turned under the hot spray of water, feeling the stink and grime of his lazy fourteen days wash down the drain. He wiped at the mirror, lathered his face up with Edge, and scraped away the accumulated red stubble there that had almost become a beard. It was good to see his own wholesome face again. He smiled.

While he had the razor in his hand, he went ahead and shaved the pubes away from his balls and then above his dick, which always made it look bigger. Who knew? Maybe he would feel inspired tonight to actually do something about the state of his celibacy. It might be nice to connect with another human being, as opposed to beating off into an athletic sock as he gazed at the fine entertainment offerings from Treasure Island Media.

He stepped from the shower, rubbed himself dry, and found he was actually looking forward to the evening.

*

"That one over there has his eye on you." Jared nodded toward a man leaning on the wall across from them.

They had ventured into several bars tonight and this one, the Eagle, Thad had never been to before. He had always been afraid it would be too rough trade for him, that he'd be laughed out of the bar for his lack of chaps and harness. But once Jared had convinced him to go, he realized the Eagle was not all that different from the other bars they had been to, and maybe, in fact, was a little better. It was certainly more low-key and less pretentious, with a handful of patrons who were older than at most of the other bars he was used to frequenting. And other than the biker jackets and combat boots here and there, the attire wasn't all that much different either. Add to that the refreshing lack of cologne, and Thad thought he might have just found a place worth returning to.

Thad followed Jared's nod and looked at the man across the bar. The man lifted his beer bottle toward him and gave a smile that was tentative, a little bit shy, and altogether charming. Like Thad, he had red hair. But his was cropped into a buzz, and he also had a full beard. He wore a simple Old Navy thermal tee that didn't hide the fact he had a bit of potbelly. Leather jacket—bomber style, not biker—and Levi's completed his ensemble. He had the audacity to be wearing sneakers. Thad thought he looked kind of cuddly and, when he probed his own intellect a little deeper, nonthreatening.

He returned the beer bottle salute and the smile. In no time Big Red was making his way across the bar toward him.

"Uh-oh, bear headed your way. Brace yourself," Jared whispered in his ear, then moved away to talk to another guy a few stools down.

God, I don't know if I'm ready for this. Thad tried to look casual, but he felt himself stiffening up inside, and not in a good way.

"Hi, I'm Kevin." The man stood before him, hand extended. Thad took it and was pleased with the firm confidence of the man's grasp.

"Thad."

"So what brings you out tonight?"

"My friend, actually." Thad thought for a minute, and then it all poured out. "He thought I needed a little night life. I've been moping around for the past couple of weeks."

Kevin took a swig of his beer and cocked his head. "Boyfriend troubles?"

"How did you know?"

"It's not hard. That's what friends do. And you have this kind of scared, sad vibe going on."

Thad wondered about that, cursing himself for having the kind of face that was read so easily. "Well, it's actually ex-boyfriend."

"That's good to hear." Kevin stepped a bit closer. He clinked his beer bottle against Thad's. "To getting back in circulation."

Is that what he was doing? From even these few minutes, he could tell Kevin was a nice guy and he was interested. He could imagine taking him home or going back to his place, even though such imaginings were way too fast. And with that imagining, Thad felt a twinge of panic. He didn't know if he was prepared for this, if he was truly over Sam. Would he close his eyes when kissing Kevin and feel Sam's beard against his chin? Would he call out Sam's name in the heat of passion? Did he really want to wake up in the morning with a stranger snoring beside him? Would that really help erase the sadness and loss?

He allowed himself to talk to Kevin for the next half hour. Found out he worked for Microsoft and still had a job—a good one, actually, as a technical writer—had moved to Seattle five years ago from Minneapolis, and liked mountain hiking when the weather permitted. Under other circumstances this was someone with whom Thad thought there might be a connection, at least a date or two. But tonight he couldn't permit himself to respond when Kevin's thigh nudged his own or to return any of the meaningful stares poor Kevin attempted to level his way.

In the end, he decided that to continue talking to Kevin would just be leading him on. As much as he thought a one-night stand might do him some good, his heart told him the time was not right. And maybe it would never be. Perhaps his connection with Sam had changed him, and now maybe hooking up was a thing of the past. Thad might have become, without even knowing it, a hopeless romantic who needed both a physical and emotional connection for intimacy to occur.

Or maybe he was just vulnerable.

So he hedged his bets a bit and had Kevin enter his phone number into his iPhone, pleading the "I gotta get up early" defense, and left him to find Jared.

Jared stood next to a short, muscular Asian man whose hair was a mass of stiff black bristles that stood straight up. He had thrown his head back in laughter, and the guy had already slid his arm around Jared's waist. Thad tapped him on the shoulder to get his attention. Jared turned to look at him and must have seen, from just the look on his face, that for Thad the evening was over.

"You ready to go?" Jared smiled, and Thad fully expected him to offer to pay for his cab—an offer he would decline; he was not *that* helpless. After all, it looked like he was in the midst of reeling in yet another hot prospect for the night. Jared was Jared...and Thad knew that going out with him often meant coming home without him.

But Jared surprised him. He turned to his new friend, and they did the same little exchange of cell phone numbers Thad had just done with Kevin. Then he grabbed Thad's arm and started to lead him to the door.

"Wait a minute! You're passing up *that*?"

"I need to see my best friend home safely. My Vespa is just up the road on Minor."

"You. Leaving a hot man behind. Wow, you could knock me over with a feather right now."

"I'd rather use a brick." Jared laughed. "Come on. It's gonna be a chilly ride home."

Once they pulled up in front of his place in Green Lake, Thad felt as if his face had frozen into position. *Note to self: never ride on the back of a Vespa in winter. It's too fuckin' cold.*

Thad slid off the seat and stomped his feet to get the blood flowing again. He wondered if the way he had clung to Jared during the ride home had been misinterpreted. Jared looked over his shoulder at Thad, seemingly unfazed by the chill. He was smiling.

"You gonna ask me in for a nightcap?"

Thad grinned back. His place was clean, fresh sheets on the bed. But was the question a loaded one? He knew, just from a few minutes alone with a new guy, that for him to have any kind of intimate involvement with someone again, he required a connection on a deeper level than just physical.

He had that with Jared.

There were all sorts of good reasons to invite Jared inside. He was hot. He was caring. He clearly held strong feelings for Thad, feelings that had only deepened over their shared recent traumas.

There were also all sorts of bad reasons too. For one thing, nothing ruined a really good friendship faster than sex. Thad had learned that lesson the hard way on more than one occasion. You might say *Oh, it'll just be a casual thing, two friends having fun*, but it never was. It always seemed, at least for Thad, to end in awkwardness and a weakening of the friendship bond that was often stronger than what any so-called relationship could offer. He wasn't sure he wanted to jeopardize that.

When would he learn the secret of combining friendship and great love?

So he simply leaned forward and gave Jared a warm, lingering kiss on the mouth, minus any tongue, to ensure his intentions were clear. "You know what? I'm not over him yet."

Jared nodded and rolled his eyes, the disappointment plain on his face. Thad understood all at once that this evening out and this ride home was about a lot more than just cheering Thad up. It was about designs and dreams Jared had as well. "And if you wanna come in for a nightcap, I have some Mount Rainier in cans, but that's about it. And that *is* about it, if you know what I mean."

Jared shrugged. "Well, if you change your mind and want me to come back, you have my number."

"Not going off to the baths?"

"Nah." Jared gave a cockeyed grin. "What I want isn't there."

Thad hugged him. "You're a good friend."

"Too good."

And with that Jared started up his bike and rode off into the night, leaving Thad to watch as he grew smaller and smaller until he finally disappeared.

Chapter Twenty

DECEMBER

She circles *around in front of the squat apartment building, sniffing the air and pawing impatiently. For her, this is not about feeding a need, satisfying a hunger.*

It is about revenge.

She paws at the ground, whines, and at last raises her head to howl at the full moon above her, a glowing pewter orb laid out on a blanket of black velvet. She doesn't care who hears her, doesn't care if she is discovered. If she has to die for vengeance, then so be it.

From between a couple of parked cars, she watches the window that's her target, anticipating the moment the light inside will be extinguished. In the dark room, her prey waits. If it weren't for him, perhaps her life would be different now. Perhaps all the tragedy wouldn't have occurred. The kill will be easier in the darkness, quicker, surer. Her superior night vision will give her an advantage. There will be no struggling, no messiness.

She so hates a mess.

And the taste of his blood will be sweet.

She returns her gaze to the warm rectangle of light. Twin tusks of steam rise from her snout.

She waits.

*

Thad wished he were tired. No, he wished he were sleepy. He was bone tired but knew sleep was an elusive thing, always hiding around this or that corner, depriving him and making him look older.

He had watched a DVD—*Humpday*, which was boring and never really delivered on its promise, several episodes of *Fringe* he had recorded—and which seemed no stranger than his own life, and had even drunk three— no, make that four—beers. Yet he still felt alert, awake, alive—all things he didn't want to feel.

He longed for the oblivion of sleep. But that particular human satisfaction had kept its charms to itself since the night Jared had dropped him off two weeks ago in front of his apartment. A sense of unfinished business— between him and Sam, between him and Jared—lay at his feet. Even when he did manage to fall into a somewhat restless slumber, he would awaken in the middle of the night, thinking about one man or the other. And each night it seemed harder and harder to drift off into that oblivious state known as slumber.

So here he sat, waiting, knowing the worst thing he could do to fall asleep was to wait, to be on guard for it. Reluctantly, he switched off the TV and stripped down to his boxers and a T-shirt. He slid into bed beside Edith, who snored contentedly atop a regular pillow and throw pillow she had arranged into a bed for herself, next to where Thad's head would eventually rest.

Just as he lay down, he realized he had forgotten to turn off the torchiere lamp next to the front door. He got up, switched it off, and stumbled back to bed, trying to revel in the comfort of flannel sheets and a goose-down comforter but only able to stare at the ceiling.

Which one should I think of first? Sam? Or Jared?

Oh, it doesn't matter. Both will keep me up until the light in the room turns gray, until my furniture begins to take on form and definition.

Thad turned onto one side, burrowing down beneath the flannel sheets, yanking the comforter up to his ears, in a position that would have—at one time—effortlessly sent him off to dreamland.

Now it felt as though his eyes were glued open.

On the one hand, Jared has always been there for me. And therein lies the problem. He's such a good friend, he's become almost like a brother. And incest scenes do not titillate me.

Thad flipped over onto his back, where he traced a hairline crack in the ceiling.

And then there is Sam. My beautiful, hotter-than-hell man. He is like a Colt fantasy come to life. He satisfies me in bed and out. He nourishes me. Again, in bed and out. He makes me laugh. He charms me with his baritone and his accent every time he opens his mouth. And when he opens his mouth to kiss me, it's like his full lips and tongue are hot-wired to my groin. And let's not even go lower...to those hard pecs, dusted with coarse black hair, the flat belly, the treasure trail leading down to his fat, thick...

Thad rolled over onto his stomach, thrusting helplessly against his sheets. He was just about to come when he heard the noise. He rolled back over and eased up on his elbows, listening. It sounded like something was clawing at his door. Edith reared up, jumped from the bed, and let loose with a hysterical chorus of yaps, running toward the door and jumping up and down in front of it as though her feet were on springs.

Thad sat up.

What was out there?

*

Getting inside the lair of her prey does present its problems. She whines, clawing at the door, and can hear she's roused the little rat living inside. She paws at the door again, her long black claws making a very satisfying screech in the cold night. The little dog inside is going crazy. She can only hope her prey is stupid enough to open the door. A tiny crack is all it would take...

And then she will be upon him, like flame upon paper. She will go first for the throat, stunning and silencing him, tasting the sharp, metallic fountain of blood that will jet forth, the sweet, savory meat of the young.

And the satisfying sensation she can only think of as justice.

She nudges her shoulder against the door's aluminum frame. She has mighty strength in her body, like coiled steel, and she knows she can break down the door if she has to. But she hopes, perversely, that she will be able to rely on the stupidity of her prey. If he were only smart enough to not open doors, perhaps she would not have to be here tonight. No, she could be off with her brothers, in the snow of the Cascades, searching for more vulnerable and less conspicuous prey.

She rams herself against the door, feeling it give a little under her weight and the power of her muscles. The dog inside at last whimpers, and she hears the click of its claws as it scampers away.

*

Thad flattened himself against the headboard as Edith gave a final desperate wail and scurried under the bed. He listened as she growled. What was out there?

Domenic, as far as Thad knew, was dead, buried in rocky soil on some hillside in Sicily. Sam, he was sure, would never threaten him. And he'd told Thad that the rest of the family never took human lives when they changed.

So what was outside, then? Was it an ordinary murderer? Robber? Psycho? Were these things any less frightening? He tried to swallow and found his throat was dry. His heart thudded uncomfortably in his chest, pounding at what seemed like three times its normal rate.

Think, Thad, think.

He eyed his cell phone, lying on the nightstand. Tentatively he picked it up and pressed the first nine, which illuminated the little keyboard. He dialed in one and then another one. When the dispatcher answered, he couldn't say anything at first, then managed to whisper, "Someone's trying to break into my apartment."

"Sir? Sir, can you tell me where you are?"

Robotically, Thad managed to get out his address and his name. "Hurry!" he squeaked as he saw the door separate from its frame.

"Just stay with me, sir. We'll get someone over to you ASAP."

Thad dropped the phone on the bed, wishing there weren't so many shoes, boxes, and porno DVDs beneath the bed so he could fit himself under there with Edith. He wished suddenly for a back door or even a window out of which he could throw himself.

But he sat paralyzed on the bed, watching the door separate farther and farther from its frame. He could hear the almost tinny squawk of the 911 dispatcher as she talked to him from the phone lying atop the sheets. What could he do? He was helpless. He could only pray the cops would get there soon enough.

But they were God knew where, and this thing trying to break into his apartment was right here and right now. The police could take long minutes to get there, time Thad might not have to spare.

The door finally gave way, and Thad stuffed a fist into his mouth, understanding for the first time what it felt like to be too terrified to scream.

A large, hulking black wolf—larger than Thad had ever seen or imagined—stood framed in the doorway, illuminated in silver by the light of the moon. Steam rose from its nostrils. Its mouth was open and drooling.

Thad's heart pounded so hard he thought it would explode inside his chest. He wanted to scream, but all he could manage was a desperate panting. He wanted to move but felt frozen, like a bug pinned to a board.

The wolf stared at him, its eyes amber and ablaze. Thad knew right at that moment they both were aware of the same thing: it would take only one leap from the wolf's muscular back legs for it to fly across the room and land on the bed with Thad. And then how long would it take for the thing to rip his throat out? Seconds? Was this how it would all end?

The two stared at one another for a long time, neither moving. And then the wolf hunched down on its powerful haunches and leaped—just like Thad's nightmarish imagination had shown him only moments before—across the room. Thad felt the thud of it landing on the bed, then found himself flattened on his back, staring up into feral eyes he once thought could only be countenanced in hell. The wolf's fangs were impossibly huge and looked razor sharp.

Thad curled onto his side, drawing his legs up to his chest, his only coherent thought a prayer that things be over quickly, that it not hurt too much. Eyes squeezed shut, he could still smell the animal's fetid breath and feel the heat radiating from its body. He whimpered.

And then everything changed. He heard a scuffle as something else entered the room. The bed weighed down once more, and then all the weight shifted off it. Growls, whines, and whimpers filled his ears. Thad opened his eyes only slightly to take in the specter of two wolves in his tiny studio now, hulking black twins facing one another in a stance Thad could only interpret as confrontational. A low growl, almost like an electrical hum, issued forth from each animal, from deep within their chests. When they weren't growling, they drew their lips back, exposing razor-sharp fangs. They restlessly pawed the floor, circling one another.

This has to be a dream. Too much has gone on in the past few months. My subconscious is simply overloaded. These nightmare images are spilling out, playing for me like the most terrifying horror movie I have ever seen. This isn't real. This is not real.

But as much as Thad told himself these things, he knew it wasn't so. The hallmarks of reality were there before him. Dreams could seem real, but they never seemed so real that they were indistinguishable from the fabric of real life. Not for Thad, anyway. He scooted back so he was flattened against the wall. For the first time in probably twenty years, he stuffed his thumb in his mouth, only dimly aware he was doing it.

He prayed the beasts would tear each other apart... and leave him the hell alone.

God, or whatever higher power kept watch, must have heard Thad, because one of the wolves leaped upon the other, snarling, its iron jaws clamping down into the other wolf's neck. The pair scuffled, rolling around, jaws snapping, letting out the occasional yelp. First one was on top, then the other. Fur flew. The smell of sweat and raw animal filled the air, like terror made into a bizarre perfume. Mixed in with the yelps, snarls, growls, barks, and howls of agony, he heard the sound of distant sirens.

Thank God. I am—I think, I hope, I pray—going to make it out of this night alive.

Speaking of the night, Thad noticed a subtle lightening outside. The sky had gone from pitch black to an almost formless gray. With that reckoning Thad sat up as one of the wolves let out a piercing wail, more akin to a human scream than anything animal, and slumped to the floor.

The other wolf stood over it, blood dripping from its fangs. It raised its head and howled, long and mournful.

Then it ran from the room.

The noise of the sirens became deafening.

How am I going to explain a giant dead wolf in the middle of my apartment? The sound of official vehicles screeching to a halt in front of his small apartment complex was near deafening. Thad rushed to leap from the bed to pull on some jeans and a sweatshirt. Edith poked her head out from beneath the bed, nose upraised to smell the coppery tang of blood in the air. He scooped her up and then cradled her close.

In the few seconds it took for Thad to dress, everything changed. The sky brightened more, into that inescapable start known as dusk.

And the wolf faded away.

In its place, Graziela lay. Her nude body stretched out, black hair a fan behind her, dark eyes staring up at a vision only she could see.

Her throat was a jagged tear from which blood now slowly trickled. The rising sun revealed blood splatters on the wall and all over Thad's furniture.

Like hoofbeats, the footsteps of cops and paramedics thundered up the front walk.

Chapter Twenty-One

"It was you, wasn't it?"

Sam eyed him from across the table. His heavy brow was furrowed, and his reddened eyes displayed his remorse and anguish unmistakably...in crimson. The way he slumped in his chair told a tale of despair better than the few words he had uttered since sitting down with Thad only a half hour or so ago.

They had the Blue Moon Café to themselves this early afternoon. Sam had closed the place, and what remained of his family was sequestered in the apartment adjacent to the restaurant—in mourning.

The Seattle police had hauled Thad into the precinct, questioned, and not quite cleared him of any suspicion in the death of Graziela Lupino.

Thad hadn't even bothered trying to tell a tale of gigantic wolves wrestling in his studio apartment. He simply told them that a man had broken in—the signs of forced entry were all too apparent—and that Graziela was with the man. The pair quarreled, and it ended violently. Thad didn't know why they had chosen his home to break into nor why they had chosen him to be a witness to their carnage. Perhaps, he suggested at one point, because Graziela knew him, she had run to his place to be saved. Exhausted and terrified, it was the best story he could come up with at the time.

He wondered if anyone could think of a more plausible explanation. He knew he faced more questions down the road, and the chance that the crime could be made to fit him. He also knew that without any other leads, he might begin to look more and more like a promising suspect, which was only one of the many reasons that, once released, the first person he'd come to see was Sam.

He repeated his question. "It was you, wasn't it?"

Sam nodded. "Of course it was me. I knew my sister. Knew how much she loved Domenic and how much she blamed me—and what I am—for what happened to him. For her loss. Because she saw it as her loss more than anyone else's.

"I knew she would come to you. She would look for someone to blame. I hoped she wouldn't harm you, but I was sure, deep down, that she would try. That's why, when the moon was full, I followed her."

Sam lowered his head and let out a strangled sob. He angrily wiped at the tears, sniffed, and raised his head. "She did everything I expected her to do. I let her go as far as she did only because I hoped she might have a little remorse, show she had a conscience, even in the state she was in. I wanted my sister to know right from wrong. I wanted my sister…" Sam let out a cry of despair. "I wanted my sister not to kill the man I love."

Thad reached across the table and covered Sam's trembling hands with his own. "I can't imagine what you feel, sweetheart. I can't imagine the place you must have been in."

"I had to protect you. And there was only one way…" Sam's voice trailed off, and he stared outside at the gray, drizzly day.

Thad had trouble wrapping his mind around the enormity of it. Sam had killed his sister to save him. *His sister*. He had just lost his son. Never mind that both were homicidal and perhaps inherently evil. They were his flesh and blood. And their otherness probably made their bonds to one another even stronger than the bonds in an ordinary family. He wondered how Sam could go on.

And he had another concern too. He felt selfish and callous for even thinking of it, but he supposed this was where self-preservation stepped in. Thad was free now, but how long would it be before that changed, before he viewed the world from behind bars? His confusion, grief, and genuine shock had made the detectives who interviewed him take his implausible story somewhat seriously. But how long would it be until they said to themselves "This guy had to have been the killer. Even if he had none of the victim's blood on him, he had to be involved. Ain't no other way it could happen."

Thad loved Sam and loved what he had done for him, the sacrifice he had made for him. But did he love him enough to take the fall for him? A fall that would effectively cut short his young life?

Maybe. Sam had sacrificed for him. Thad could sacrifice for Sam.

But he didn't know if he could be that generous. He had to say the words. "My love, I don't know how to put this... There's a very real chance I could be blamed for what happened to Graziela. I could be put away...forever. It happened in my house, right in front of me. As far as the police knew, there was no one else around. My story is full of holes." Thad covered his face with his hands, then dropped them to Sam, his eyes shimmering with tears. "What are we gonna do?"

"Would you be willing to leave all you know behind?" Sam had never looked more serious.

"What do you mean?" Even though he had asked the question, Thad felt he already knew the answer.

"Before I answer that question, let me ask you one more. And it's important. Do you think what I did was wrong?" Sam sat back, locking gazes with Thad.

Graziela would have killed Thad if Sam had not stopped her. He didn't think there were any other alternatives or half measures that would have worked. Sam had acted purely in Thad's defense, at great and unimaginable loss to himself. Thad shook his head, sorrowful. "No, of course I don't. You saved me. We both know she would have killed me if you hadn't been there. If I could have killed her myself, I would have. But she was too strong for me."

"You are right. So I must ask you again. Are you willing to leave all you know behind?"

Thad cocked his head as if he pondered the question, but he knew what Sam was asking. Could he leave everything behind? Seattle? His family in Chicago? *Jared?* There was a certain mad appeal to running off with Sam, to creating a whole new life for himself with the man he loved. But this seemed to Thad a once-in-a-lifetime decision. There could be no turning back. If he ran away with Sam and things cooled after a while, or if Sam's full-moon habits became too strange for even him, Thad would be alone in a strange country, where he didn't even know the language.

"I know what you're thinking, Sam. And part of me wants to grab you and hold you and shout *yes, yes, yes!* But even with all that's happened, even with all the love I feel for you—and it's a lot—I don't know. I don't know if I can just vanish from this life. *My* life. I don't know if I can leave the people I love behind. I worry, too, the police might view me leaving the country as very suspicious." Thad's head drooped. "I don't know if I love you that much."

He looked up at Sam then, afraid he would be angry, but saw only compassion in the man's features.

"Maybe," Sam whispered, "we talk too much." He stood, walked over to Thad, stooped, and gathered a surprised Thad into his arms, as if Thad were nothing more than a small child. The pair walked wordlessly toward the back.

Sam headed straight for his bedroom. He set Thad gently on the unmade bed, closed and locked the door, and drew the shades against the dull gray light outside. Thad watched as Sam undressed, exposing the perfectly sculpted chest dusted with coarse black hair, the cobbled stomach, and when he removed his pants, the massive thighs...in the center of which Sam's manhood jutted, already erect and dripping precum. Thad gasped, lay back, and struggled quickly out of his own clothes.

They came together like a collision, like a silken explosion. Sam's mouth and tongue found Thad's and practically devoured him, his hunger undeniable. At the same time, Sam positioned himself between Thad's spread thighs and slid slowly inside. It hurt, but Thad would not, could not have stopped him for anything. In only moments the pain gave way to delirious pleasure, and Thad found himself bucking to meet Sam's frantic, starving thrusts. Their mouths never unlocked. And it was over in minutes. It wasn't until they lay in each other's arms that Thad realized cum was not the only bodily fluid covering them.

There were tears too.

Thad stroked the hair on Sam's chest, burying his fingers in it. How could he say goodbye to this?

How could he not?

And so, as the light faded in the room, Thad began to tell Sam of his decision...and his plan.

"I love you. I think I always will. But I can't give myself, my life, up for you. Perhaps one day this...this tragedy will all blow over. You can come back. And we will see where we stand then."

Sam didn't look at him. He stared up at the ceiling. "Don't. Don't do this. I have lost so much."

"You have, but it's not just about you, sweetheart. It's about both of us. And our differences are great. Who's to say that once the passion wears off—and it always does, except in fairy tales or romance novels—those differences won't set us farther apart? And then where will we be?"

Stubbornly Sam said, "I will make you happy. I will work every day to make you happy."

"I know you will. And I would do the same." Thad sighed, rolling over on his side, facing away from Sam. "I just can't do this. Not like this. Not in the heat of this despair and passion. I need a level head. I need my family too. You should understand that."

This last line must have gotten to Sam because he said sadly, "I know. I ask too much."

The room continued to darken as they lay in silence. There really were no more words to be spoken. After what seemed like a very long time, Sam began talking again. "I have to leave, though. I must go home."

"I know. I understand."

Sam let out a long, trembling sigh that foretold tears. He took in several quick breaths. "But I will not—as they say—throw you to the wolves."

Surprisingly, both laughed, and not just for a short time. When they had calmed down, Sam continued. "I will leave soon—today. But you must not take the blame for what I had to do. We both agree it wasn't wrong, but other forces won't see it that way. You must go to the authorities and tell them I killed my sister."

"Why?"

"You know why. Because you will be blamed. We both know. Most likely they are already building a case against you."

Thad silently conceded the point.

"You tell them I did it. You tell them the truth. That Graziela came to kill you and I stepped in to defend you. The fact that she was naked could be explained away by the fact that she wanted to keep her clothes free of blood. You don't have to tell about our other selves." Sam was quiet for a while. He added, "My blood is there as well—at the, how do you say it, scene of the crime."

"What if they don't believe me?" That very real fear caused Thad's pulse to quicken.

"Don't you watch *CSI*? *Bones*?"

Thad laughed. The question seemed so out in left field. "I don't know what you mean."

"There are people, experts, I forget what they're called. I do not know the name in English. They find evidence, process it."

"A medical examiner? Forensics?"

"That sounds right. You tell these people I did it. As I said, the proof is there...my blood, my fingerprints, my hair. It will all match up. It will make a convincing case."

"And if they ever come looking for you?"

Sam's voice was grave. "They will never find me."

Neither will I.

The thought just about broke his heart. Thad bit his lower lip hard enough to taste his own blood. He got up from the bed and looked down at his beautiful man lying spread-eagled, twisted up in the sheets, and glazed with a light coat of sweat.

He kissed him. "I love you. I hope—someday, somehow—you will come back to me."

"I want only that." Sam let a breath escape. "I am going to close my eyes now. When I open them again, I think it will be easier for us both if you are not here."

Quietly, quickly, Thad dressed and left the Blue Moon Café...forever.

Chapter Twenty-Two

Capitol Hill at dusk looked inviting. The light had faded to an almost lavender hue, and warm yellow lights appeared in the windows of the large old brick homes and apartment buildings.

Thad walked for a long time along the streets of the neighborhood, heading over to where the streets sloped downward with views of downtown, the mountains, and of course, the Space Needle.

Eventually, he ended up on Aloha. It was as though all the meandering had a purpose—to bring him here. Ahead was the redbrick apartment building that only a mere couple of weeks before had been the scene of carnage and a media circus.

As he neared the building, something made him look up at one of the windows.

Jared stared down at him. And then disappeared from view.

As Thad stared up the walkway, the front door squeaked open and Jared emerged, smiling. He looked terrific in a pair of ripped-up jeans, hiking boots, and a worn flannel shirt.

"Hey, stranger," he called out. "Lookin' for trouble?"

Thad hurried up the walk toward Jared. It felt like coming home.

And yet... And yet...

As he neared Jared's open doorway, he felt as though he were being pulled forward *and* backward at the very same time. He stood, frozen on the threshold.

Jared opened the door wider and cocked his head. "Coming in?" He smiled, and his gaze locked with Thad's.

Thad stepped inside, feeling suddenly nervous, out of sorts, and a little sick. On his way over here, he'd been so sure what he'd wanted. He'd thought: *I love Jared. He and I are like two peas in a pod. In a way, we're like two halves of a whole. He gets me and I him. There may not be a blazing fire here, but there's a spark. Just look at his cute little face! In time, our love will grow.*

He sat on Jared's worn couch, and one of his dogs came over, tail wagging, to be petted. Thad absentmindedly patted the dog's head and scratched behind his ears, staring all the while out the window at the muted violet light.

Jared was saying something, and only just now did Thad realize it. He shifted his gaze to his friend, his best friend. "What?" he asked dully.

Jared laughed. "Coffee? I just made some. Should I pour you a mug? Or is it too late for the likes of you?" Jared snickered. "I have beer too—and the harder stuff." He winked.

Thad let out a quivering sigh. "No, I don't want anything."

Jared sat down beside him. "Dude, what's wrong? You seem a million miles away."

"Is that how far it is to Sicily?" Thad wondered.

"What?"

Thad shook his head. "I was all set to come over here and give myself to you, I suppose." He grinned as Jared raised his eyebrows.

"I have a feeling that's not gonna happen," Jared said.

Thad shook his head. "No. And by *give myself*, I mean in a bigger context. As in boyfriend, partner, potential husband."

Jared laughed. "And you decided that I'd accept? All on your own? Do I have a say here?" Jared nudged Thad's shoulder with his own. "I love you, buddy, but I'm not ready to settle down." He took Thad's face in his hands. "You're very special to me, man. No doubt. But we're a lot like brothers..." he trailed off.

"I know. But I thought maybe we could make things work. If we gave it a try..."

"What are you talking about? We're buds, BFFs. Right?"

Thad nodded. Should he let Jared in on everything that had transpired during the night? Of course he would, but something in him told him now was not the time. Now was the time to tell him something he was starting to know more and more, not in his head but in his heart.

"You were my safety net," Thad said. "But life isn't about clinging to safety nets. It's about leaping and trusting that the net will appear, or at least so I've heard."

"I don't know what the hell you're talking about."

And he said it, all at once. "I'm moving to Sicily with Sam. Right away." As soon as the words were out, he felt as though a great weight had been lifted from his shoulders. Deep within, he knew *this* was the real answer. He could feel it not only in his bones but in his blood, his skin, his scalp, taste it on his tongue. A sense of relief, almost palpable, rushed through him.

His love for Sam was real. And if he didn't follow him *home*, Thad knew he'd regret it for the rest of his life.

Jared laughed. "You're what?"

"Sam's leaving the country. He wants me to come with him. At first I thought I couldn't do it, thought I couldn't leave the people I love—like you, like my family—but I realized that maybe we don't always get a second chance at love. Maybe we only find our great dark man once." Thad stared off into the distance. "I've found mine." He turned back to Jared. "And I need to be with him, wherever he goes. I have to follow this, see where it leads. Maybe it'll be the best thing I've ever done, or maybe it will be the worst, but if I'm afraid of making a mistake, if I have this fear of failure, I'll never grow."

Thad stopped for a moment. "And maybe I'll never love...again."

Jared said softly, "Oh, come on, Thad. There are plenty of fish in the sea." He winked. "I can attest to that."

Thad nodded. "But there's only one Sam."

"You're really going to do it, aren't you?" Jared looked sad, his eyes a little misty. His next words were a contradiction, but Thad knew he meant them and loved Jared even more for saying them. "I'm happy for you."

Thad stood up, feeling suddenly energized. "I need to go."

Jared chuckled. "To Sicily? Right now?"

"You think I'm kidding, but Sam's leaving soon, maybe as soon as tomorrow, and I need to be with him."

"Why the urgency?"

And at last Thad told him everything that had happened through the night and into the early morning. His friend, more than anyone else in the world, would understand, would know he wasn't spinning some far-out paranormal tale but speaking the truth.

"Wow" was all Jared could say.

Thad stooped down to kiss Jared on the lips. "I'll always love you, man. And I hope one day we'll see each other again."

"I hear Sicily's beautiful." Jared turned away, and Thad suspected it was to hide his tears.

"I'll be in touch when I get settled, okay?"

"Sure you will." Jared still couldn't look at him.

Thad hurried from the apartment, not sure if Jared's final words to him were sarcastic or heartfelt. He wasn't sure himself if he'd ever see this wonderful man again.

He hoped so.

But right now Sam, his love, was out there, and he needed to catch him before he was gone.

Chapter Twenty-Three

They sat on one of the biggest boulders along the rocky shoreline. Before them stretched the churning waters of the Mediterranean. In the darkness its whitecaps stood out as the waves crashed against the rocks, sending up spray that every so often splashed Sam and Thad, cooling them and making them laugh. The water itself looked almost black, but not quite, imbued with a deep navy color. On the surface of the water, the reflection of the moon, nearly full, stretched and contracted.

Under the blanket draped over both pairs of shoulders, they were naked. On that same blanket, spread out on the even-at-night hot sand, they'd made love. Like the rush of the sea before them now, the sex had surged and retreated, rough and then calm.

This was their quiet spot, the place they could get away from Sam's family and truly, as Thad put it, "howl at the moon."

Thad put his head on Sam's shoulder. He smelled of sweat and smoke, and Thad lightly stroked Sam's bicep.

"Are you still glad you came with me? Not missing Seattle too much?"

Thad closed his eyes. The answer to the two questions didn't align perfectly. This wasn't, after all, a fairy tale. "Oh, I miss a lot about America and the people I left there." Thad laughed. "Thank God we managed to get Edith over here!" He shook his head, thinking of how the dog loved the Sicilian air and sunshine. Thad shook his head. "But I can't deny the things and people I miss and probably always will. But am I glad I traveled across the world to be with you? Oh yes, of course. I might miss home—I mean Seattle, America—but I don't ever have any regrets."

"Because you're with the man you love?"

"Because I'm with the man I love."

Sam squeezed him, pulling Thad closer, a feat that until a moment ago Thad wouldn't have thought possible.

For a long time, they sat in comfortable silence, staring out at the sea. Then Sam reached down and lifted a small plastic container out of the bag on the boulder at their feet. Inside were cold artichokes, marinated in olive oil, garlic, and red pepper. Sam had made an aioli from eggs and Parmigiano-Reggiano and, of course, more garlic. He fed one to Thad by hand.

Thad closed his eyes in revelatory pleasure. He let the artichoke and its pungent dip linger and dance on his taste buds. "You know the only reason I followed you here, right?"

"My big dick?" Sam asked, laughing.

"Well, there's that. But it's your cooking, really, that keeps me by your side."

Sam shook his head and fed him another heart.

They both stared up at the moon, right now partially obscured by a slate gray strand of cloud passing by.

"Soon," Thad whispered.

And Sam nodded. "*Sì*. But you know I won't harm anyone."

Thad nodded and stared into Sam's brown eyes, loving the curious mixture of gentleness and ferocity he knew mingled there.

"Let's not think about that right now," Sam said.

"Let's think about us," Thad agreed. He reached down for another heart and fed it to Sam.

"Two hearts," Sam said softly.

Lupino Family Favorite Recipes

Note from the author: *Sam and Thad wanted me to share these recipes with you. Enjoy… during a full moon or not!*

Ricotta-stuffed Arancini*

(Rice balls, in Italian: *arancini di riso con ricotta*. Arancini in Italian means oranges, or what these look like when fried up).

INGREDIENTS

Salt and pepper to taste

4 cups water

1 cup bread crumbs, preferably homemade (if using store-bought, don't get the flavored variety)

2 tablespoons olive oil, plus more for frying

1/2 cup ricotta cheese, preferably full-fat, both for flavor and consistency

2 teaspoons chopped fresh thyme

1 1/4 cups arborio rice (the kind you use in risotto)

Flour, for dredging

1/4 cup dry white wine

2 large eggs, beaten

Zest of a lemon

1/2 small onion, minced

1 tablespoon freshly grated Parmigiano-Reggiano

DIRECTIONS

Heat the 2 tablespoons of olive oil in a medium saucepan (a minute or two). Add onion and cook over medium/low until soft and fragrant—don't burn! Pour in your rice and raise the heat a bit. Stir rice until it's coated with oil and sizzling, a couple of minutes. Add in the wine and simmer until evaporated, about three minutes. Add water and bring to a boil. Simmer, stirring every few minutes, until the water has been absorbed and the rice is tender, about twenty minutes. Take rice off the stove, add to a bowl, and let it cool.

Stir the thyme and lemon zest into the rice and season with salt and pepper. In a small bowl, blend the ricotta with the Parmigiano and season with salt and pepper. Wet your palm and grab a small handful of the rice mixture and form into a ball. Make a dent in the center and fill it with about one teaspoon of the ricotta mixture. Fold the rice around the filling to enclose it and pat the rice into a ball. Repeat with what's left.

In a medium fry pan, heat 2 inches of olive oil over medium heat. Set a rack over a large baking sheet. Put the flour, eggs, and bread crumbs in 3 separate bowls. Dredge the rice ovals in the flour, shaking off any excess. Dip the ovals in the egg; then coat with the bread crumbs. Deep-fry four ovals at a time until golden brown, a couple of minutes. With a slotted spoon, move the arancini to the rack to drain while you fry the rest. Serve hot or at room temperature.

Orecchiette Pasta Aioli with Flaked Red Pepper*

(In Italian, orecchiette means "small ear." Take a look at the pasta and you'll see why. This is a very simple but very delicious recipe!)

INGREDIENTS

16-oz. orecchiette pasta, preferably fresh, but dried is good too—as long as you stick to semolina

Handful of salt

1/4 cup olive oil

1/4 cup salted butter

1 anchovy (optional but lovely)

6 cloves fresh garlic, minced

1/2 to 1 teaspoon of red pepper flakes

1/4 to 1/2 cup grated Parmigiano-Reggiano cheese

DIRECTIONS

Put a large pot of water on the stove to boil. When it starts to bubble, add in a good handful of salt. You want it to taste like the sea! Add in pasta, cook to al dente, and reserve some of the liquid the pasta cooked in.

When pasta is almost done, heat fry pan over medium heat. Add in butter, olive oil, and if using, anchovy (this is the cured anchovy in oil, not fresh). The anchovy will melt into the oils. When butter has lost its foam, add in garlic and a sprinkle of salt. Cook, stirring, over low heat until fragrant. Don't let it brown! It will become bitter.

At this point, add in your pasta and toss with butter, oil, and garlic to coat. Add in a bit (1/4 of a cup or so) of the pasta cooking water. This will add creaminess to the sauce. Stir in red pepper flakes and grated cheese.

Serve hot! With breath mints!

Pasta Fagioli*

(This will warm your tummy and your heart on a cold day.)

INGREDIENTS

1 cup elbow macaroni

2 tablespoons olive oil, divided

1 lb. spicy Italian sausage, loose (not in casing)

4 cloves garlic, minced

1 onion, diced

3 carrots, peeled and diced

2 stalks celery, diced

3 cups chicken broth

1 (16-ounce) can tomato sauce

1 (15-ounce) can diced tomatoes, choose good quality

1 teaspoon each dried basil and dried oregano

3/4 teaspoon dried thyme

Salt and freshly ground black pepper, to taste

2 (15-ounce) cans cannellini beans (or other hearty white bean), drained and rinsed

DIRECTIONS

In a large pot of boiling salted water, cook pasta according to package instructions, drain, and set aside.

Heat 1 tablespoon olive oil in a large stockpot or Dutch oven over medium heat. Add Italian sausage to the skillet and cook until browned, about 3-5 minutes, making sure to crumble the sausage as it cooks. Drain and set aside.

Add remaining 1 tablespoon oil to the stockpot. Stir in garlic, onion, carrots, and celery. Cook, stirring occasionally, until tender, about 3-4 minutes.

Whisk in chicken broth, tomato sauce, diced tomatoes, basil, oregano, thyme, Italian sausage, and 1 cup water. Season with salt and pepper to taste. Bring to a boil. Reduce heat and simmer, covered, until vegetables are tender, about 10-15 minutes.

Stir in pasta and beans until heated through. Serve hot with some good, crusty bread.

Anise Biscotti*

(Great with your morning coffee!)

INGREDIENTS

3 1/2 cups flour

1 1/4 cups sugar

2 1/2 tablespoons baking powder

1 teaspoon anise oil

6 large eggs

2 sticks butter, melted but not hot

1 egg, beaten, for brushing on top of dough

DIRECTIONS

Sift together flour, sugar, and baking powder. Make a well in the center of the dry ingredients.

Whisk eggs until frothy. Add melted butter and anise oil.

Pour wet ingredients into dry and combine thoroughly.

On a well-floured board, put four heaping tablespoons of dough. Roll out lightly. Place on greased cookie sheet. Pat mixture down to about ¼ inch thick. Can fit up to three on a large cookie sheet (makes about five rolls). Brush top with beaten egg before putting in the oven.

Bake at 350 degrees for 25-30 minutes. When the rolls are slightly cooled, cut in 1-inch slices. Place face down and lightly toast in oven on both sides.

About the Author

Real Men. True Love.

Rick R. Reed is an award-winning and bestselling author of more than fifty works of published fiction. He is a Lambda Literary Award finalist. *Entertainment Weekly* has described his work as "heartrending and sensitive." *Lambda Literary* has called him: "A writer that doesn't disappoint..." Find him at www.rickrreedreality.blogspot.com. Rick lives in Palm Springs, CA, with his husband, Bruce, and their fierce Chihuahua/Shiba Inu mix, Kodi.

Email: rickrreedbooks@gmail.com

Facebook: www.facebook.com/rickrreedbooks

Twitter: @rickrreed

Other NineStar books by this author

Also Available from NineStar Press

Connect with NineStar Press

www.ninestarpress.com

www.facebook.com/ninestarpress

www.facebook.com/groups/NineStarNiche

www.twitter.com/ninestarpress

www.ingramcontent.com/pod-product-compliance
Lightning Source LLC
Chambersburg PA
CBHW061602100726
47898CB00002B/484